O

The Space

"Captain, sensors

information," Marsha[...] appears there are two planets revolving around the Alpha Centauri binary. No data on planet size yet. We're too far away. But the most startling information is this," he added. He punched a button on the console before him. The screen was filled with a picture of a rocky, barren asteroid.

"Well, what is it?" Traynor asked.

"It appears to be an artificially constructed planet-oid. Notice the smooth contours, the unnatural roundness of the structure. Definitely not natural."

"Fine. What does it do?" Traynor said impatiently.

"It appears, sir," Marshall explained, "to be a sensor-jamming device to prevent the locating of the planets within. It appears this device gives off the radiation that we ran into earlier. Possibly designed to keep unsuspecting visitors away."

"Let me get this straight," Commander Svenson said. "This thing is man-made?"

"Artificially created," Marshall replied. "We don't know if the creatures that created this are, in fact, human."

"But if they can hide their home planets from our sensors," Goldman asked, "why can't they hide their ships?"

"I can only guess," Marshall said, "that the equip-ment used must be immense, and they have not developed a way of miniaturizing it to a size useful on a starship."

POLARIS

SHELDON PERKINS

BELMONT TOWER BOOKS • NEW YORK CITY

A BELMONT TOWER BOOK

Published by

Tower Publications, Inc.
Two Park Avenue
New York, N.Y. 10016

I

The dining room of the transport was alive with activity. Dignitaries being transported home brushed elbows with Fleet personnel shipping out to their new posts. A blond officer of medium height stepped through the automatic doors. He surveyed the crowd with a quick glance, and was about to leave when he heard himself being paged from across the room.

"Captain Traynor," the voice called. "Captain, please join me."

Alexander Traynor looked around in an effort to discover which body belonged to the voice. Being called Captain had thrown him. He had not quite associated himself with his new rank.

Traynor quickly located the source of the voice. It turned out to be the commander of the transport, Colonel Paul Mason. The young captain had met Mason earlier, when he'd boarded the ship. Now Mason was motioning him to join the ship's officers for dinner. Traynor slid into the proffered seat and spoke his order into the computer terminal at the center of the table.

"Glad you could join us Captain," Mason said.

" 'Preciate the offer, Colonel," Traynor replied. "It's quite crowded. I hadn't realized there would be this many passengers."

"The name's Paul, sir," said Mason. "I get enough of the formalities when I'm on duty. And the crowd is mostly from Eta Barnard, sir."

"Make it Alex," Traynor grinned. "So what's the big deal about Eta Barnard?"

"Haven't you heard? They've petitioned for independence and applied for a seat on the Interplanetary Council," the Colonel replied.

"Really? " Traynor asked in amazement. "Was it accepted?"

"The Council was dismissed before a vote could be taken."

"If they vote independence, that'll make twenty-one seats on the council," Traynor said.

"That's right," Mason agreed. "Six from the Barnard system," he added. Traynor nodded, knowing the star system well.

Science took man to the stars in the twenty-first century. Space travel became a reality. But, when man was set to go, the question was raised: Where should he go? Should the first exploratory craft go to man's nearest neighbor, or should it be bypassed for a more conventional star. Both sides argued their points, but in the end, the scientists in favor of bypassing Alpha Centauri won out. Their reasons were twofold.

Reason number one involved the scientific evidence supporting the existence of a planet revolving around Barnard's Star, a star approximately 5.9 light years from Earth. Where one planet was found, there was a high probability others could be found. Possibly life could be found there.

Reason number two lay in the fact that Alpha Centauri was, in reality, a trinary. If planets did circle Alpha Centauri, no life could exist under the adverse solar conditions.

The choice of Barnard's Star had proved to be an excellent one. By 2325, over one hundred and thirty years earlier, fourteen planets had been discovered.

Eleven proved to have Earth-type atmospheres, excellent for colonization, and ten had been colonized soon after their discovery. In addition, a small planet with a methane gas atmosphere became a mining colony when it was discovered the planet was largely made up of neutronium, an essential element for the super-light neutronium drive.

The eleventh Earth-type planet was not colonized because it was found to have what scientists had hoped to find when selecting Barnard's Star for exploration: Life. The inhabitants, small stocky creatures similar in many respects to humans, were entering their atomic age when the first United Space Republic (then United Earth Republic) spaceships made contact.

After almost fifty years of UER contact, Pronetha—as her inhabitants caller their world—along with four Earth-colonized worlds, petitioned for seats on the Interplanetary Council. Pronetha, Vendra, Collier, Drina, and Mimnon were admitted to the Interplanetary Council, and the United Earth Republic was changed to the United Space Republic. Now, almost two hundred years since the other Barnard planets had received their council seats, a young planet wished to take its place in the galaxy.

"I understand that the reason for the dismissal was the reluctance of Earth to cast its vote," Mason continued. "Opposition from members of the Earth embassy who represent the Earth First party. They're a minority in Earth's embassy to the IC, but large enough to have some control over Earth's vote. Without Earth voting, Europa, Ganymede, Io, Isis, Lunar, Osiris, Titan, and Titania refused to vote. The council lost its quorum and was dismissed."

"Well, the Earth First party rears its ugly head again," Traynor said.

"Even though they lost the planetary election last

year, they keep growing in power,'' Mason told him. ''The Barnard planets are working hard for Eta's admittance. It's felt that if a council vote were taken now, nine members would vote for admittance. Against admittance, the actual tally is unknown, but at least five. Earth is the key. How she votes is how the other four will vote. With at least thirteen votes needed to pass, the Barnard planets need at least four of the six uncommitteds.'

''Tell me, Paul,'' Traynor asked. ''How are you able to gain such firsthand knowledge of council action?''

''Well, Alex,'' Mason grinned. ''On my layover at Hercules, I stayed with my brother, as I always do.'' He paused, theatrically. ''He's a member of the Earth embassy.''

Hercules, Traynor knew, was the huge, man-made asteroid that served as Fleet Command headquarters and headquarters for the USR Interplanetary Council. He laughed, thinking of how hard security was watched, and this young Fleet officer knew as much, if not more, about what was going on in the IC than many of the delegates.

''Paul,'' Traynor asked. ''Do you have any political conflicts between crew members?''

''No, not to speak of,'' replied Mason. ''Though there are fifty Earthers in my crew of one-seventy, only two are practicing members of that infernal Earth First party. They tried to recruit members of the crew when they first joined us, but I encouraged them to keep their political views to themselves while on board.''

''Encouraged?''

''I suggested that for the good of the ship, it would not be acceptable for them to cause problems among the crew, which expressing their political affiliation, and attempting to persuade others to their way of thinking, was likely to cause.''

"I take it they followed your suggestion."

"To a T," Mason answered.

"I appreciate your filling me in on the news," Traynor said. "I just got in from Sirius yesterday and was shipped out today. I found out I had been promoted to Captain by reading my new orders."

The others at the table had been diplomatically quiet, allowing the two Fleet officers to converse without interruption. Now a young lieutenant spoke up.

"Captain, what's the Sirius system like, sir?"

"Henson," Mason said, "is on his first space mission. Just graduated from the academy a month ago. He asks a lot of questions."

"That's good," Traynor observed. "Shows he's making an effort. It's the ones who don't ask questions you have to worry about." Traynor turned his chair to face the young man.

"I've been in the Sirius system for three tours of duty. Commanded *Gerinomo.* Fastest scout ship in the fleet. Also, I was weapons officer on *Francis Watkins* during the battle of Sirius.

"But to answer your question. From your studies, you must know that Sirius is a binary. The major star in the binary is a blue giant. Its companion is a white dwarf. The combination gives off a blue-white light, which takes a while to get used to. It's not bad, but when you're accustomed to the golden white of Sol, Sirius can be unsettling."

"And those blinking Earthers think they can get away with this," a man at the next table said loudly. The speaker was a minor official in the Eta Barnard political envoy. Mason threw a troubled glance in the man's direction. Traynor continued speaking, ignoring the loud remarks.

"There are ten known planets in the Sirius system. Their first planet is as far out as Jupiter in our system. Any closer and the heat from the two stars would turn the surface into liquid. As is, the sun side temperature is a constant eighty-five degrees centigrade."

"Earthers suffer from acute egomania. They think themselves indispensible to the galaxy," the Etan said, intentionally loud this time. "The higher the position they hold, the more important they think they are!"

Mason began to rise. Traynor saw his movement and shook his head. The colonel settled back into his seat uncomfortably.

"Osiris. Now there's a beautiful planet," Traynor continued. "I was there on R and R once."

"Where, sir?" a young commander asked. "I spent a week in a coastal city on the continent of Dravia."

"I had hoped to get over to Dravia, but I was occupied in a small city on Bralar."

"Occupied, sir?" Henson asked. "How?"

"Henson!" Mason said, grinning. The others laughed and the young man blushed a brilliant red.

"Excuse me, sir," Henson stammered. "I didn't mean to pry into your affairs." The others at the table, barely recovered from Henson's initial mistake, were thrown into fits by his newest slip. Henson, realizing what he had said, blushed even brighter.

"Apology noted and accepted, Lieutenant," Traynor laughed. He began eating, only to be interrupted almost immediately by the Etan at the next table.

"You there. In the fancy uniform," the man said loudly. The room grew silent. "I see by your shoulder patch that you're an Earther."

"Is he talking to me?" Traynor asked Mason, looking up from his meal. He was the only officer in dress whites. The others wore the uniform of the day, a dark blue work uniform.

"I think so," Mason replied. Traynor turned to the man.

"Were you speaking to me?" he asked politely.

"I was, Earther," the man replied savagely. "We were discussing your home planet's political stand against new members being admitted to the Interplanetary Council. We felt it might be interesting to learn an Earther's opinion on the point in question."

"My opinion," Traynor said thoughtfully. Several minutes passed. The room was silent. It seemed that everyone in the room was waiting for Traynor's answer.

"Come now," the Etan said at last. "Tell us. Everyone is waiting."

"Oh yes, my opinion," Traynor replied slowly. "You must forgive me. My mind wandered. For some reason I was thinking of the planet Osirus." A stifled laugh sounded from behind him. Traynor sympathized with Henson. He himself was having difficulty suppressing a smile. "My opinion? I have none."

"Surely you don't expect us to believe that," the man said angrily. A companion attempted to quiet the belligerent fellow by placing a hand on his shoulder. The angry man shook the hand away. "You have an opinion. Tell us! Or aren't you capable of expressing it?" he finished sarcastically.

"I'm sorry to disappoint you, but I have no opinion on the subject," Traynor replied quietly. "However, if you would like me to voice an opinion on something, I will." Traynor turned back to his plate. "This is a delicious meal," he said loudly.

Paul Mason had remained quiet when Traynor mentioned Osirus. However, this time he was unable to keep a straight face. He broke up. Nor was he the only one. Most of the diners were openly laughing at the discomfort of the diplomat.

The angry Etan rose quickly and stepped over to Traynor's seat. Gripping the other's shoulder, the Etan spun the man around to face him.

"You can't make a fool of me like that!" the Etan

cried angrily.

"I don't have to," Traynor replied. "You're doing a fine job of it yourself." The listeners applauded Traynor's last remark.

"However," Traynor said, rising. He was no longer smiling. Even though he was only medium height, Traynor stood several inches taller than the Etan. "I will no longer tolerate this harassment. If you wish to discuss something, I will listen. I will not be a party to a shouting match, though."

Traynor sat down and continued his meal. The diplomat, conspicuous to the crowd as he remained standing, looked around for a friendly face, but saw none. Angrily, the man stormed out of the dining room.

"You handled that nicely, Alex," Mason said.

"I do hope the fellow wasn't hurt," Traynor said, laughing. "Now, Isis: very similar to Osiris from what I could see from space."

Traynor settled comfortably into one of the chairs in his cabin aboard the transport. He opened the first of several folders that were piled on the table beside him. The folder he held was titled: OPERATIONAL STATUS—USRFC POLARIS.

That very morning, he had received the folders, along with his new orders. Traynor had been called into Fleet Admiral Harrington's office at 0800 hours SET (Standard Earth Time).

"Good morning, Colonel," she had said, smiling. She immediately handed him the sealed packet which he knew contained new orders. He broke the seal and lifted the flap to confirm, according to regulation procedure, that the orders were for him. On the inside of the flap would be the name and rank of the person the orders were for. He glaned at the flap and a look of surprise crossed his face.

"Ma'am, I believe there's something wrong," Traynor had said. "These orders are for Captain Alexander Traynor."

"There's nothing wrong," she replied. She slid her desk drawer open and removed a small packet. She dumped the contents onto her desktop. Out slid a full braid and two captain's bars. "Congratulations, Captain Traynor," she finished, still smiling.

Traynor accepted the envelope the Admiral handed him. He returned the braid and bars to it, then closed the flap. Harrington motioned for him to take a seat and continue reading through his orders.

Inside the packet was one sheet of paper which stated his orders plainly: Proceed to Mimnon base and assume command of the Fleet Cruiser *Polaris*.

"Is this all, ma'am?" Traynor wanted to know.

"Isn't that enough?" she replied. "You won't need any more. *Polaris* is in for repairs. Quite a few, from what I understand. She was disabled in a skirmish near Alpha Barnard. Free-floated for two days with no power except life support. Finally a destroyer discovered her and radioed for help. *Guantanamo Bay* towed her in."

"I see," Traynor said. "Is there anything special about *Polaris* I should know?"

"We all have our contacts," she smiled. "I'm no exception. From what I hear, there was a morale problem on the ship. The details are a little sketchy, so I won't feed you the rumors. However, I do know that the catalyst lay among the senior officers: captain, exec, chief surgeon, science officer, chief engineer, pilot, and navigation. The captain was bumped upstairs. Surgeon given a job on an orbital station. The rest are still there. They all survived the incident at Alpha Barnard. A lot of good people didn't." She finished solemnly.

"I see."

"You'll be interested to know that *Polaris* is being fitted with the High Energy Heat Ray," Harrington continued, in a much more conversational voice. "One of the last cruisers to be fitted."

They had spoken for a few minutes more, and then he had left. A cabin had been reserved on a military transport, which he had caught, though just barely.

Now he was reading over the operational reports of the *Polaris*. Page one, under the heading status. One word, which said it all: NONOPERATIONAL. The rest of the report was mere paper.

Traynor turned the page and came to the first section report. Engineering. A brief, non-technical, explanation of the damage to the neutronium drive. A disruptor beam had struck the engineering section, causing a chain-reaction explosion in the neutronium pile. A scientific description of what had occurred followed. Then the list of repairs to be made. Traynor skipped it for the moment. He had plenty of time on the fourteen-day trip to Mimnon.

The next report dealt with the shipboard computer. It had been totally destroyed. A new system was being installed.

The door buzzer sounded to break his concentration.

"Come," Traynor said. He closed the report as the cabin door slid open. An elderly man in a red business suit of silken material entered.

"You are Captain Alexander Traynor." It was a statement and not a question. Traynor nodded, rising. The man was ten centimeters shorter than Traynor, but in weight, edged Traynor's seventy-five kilos by an easy twenty-five kilos.

"I am Akamel Dralar, diplomatic envoy from the colony Larandra, known on star charts as Eta Barnard, to the Interplanetary Council of the United Space

Republic." The man bowed slightly. "I am here to apologize for one of the members of my party. Dratvin Pasteur is young and not experienced in the matters of interplanetary diplomacy."

"There is no need to apologize, sir," Traynor told the man. "No offense taken, and the only inconvenience was my being in the middle of my meal."

"I have spoken with Pasteur and feel he will be no more problem," Drakar said. The entrance buzzer sounded again.

"Come."

The door opened and a dark-haired young man stepped into the cabin. He wore a white Fleet uniform with clusters and the insignia of the medical corps on his collar.

"Excuse me, sir," the officer said, with the trace of a French accent. "I didn't know you were busy." He started to leave.

"That's quite all right, young man," Dralar said, smiling. "I was just leaving." He turned to Traynor. "Good evening." Traynor nodded to the man. Dralar exited with the doctor's eyes on him. The medic turned back to Traynor.

"I hope I didn't interrupt anything important, sir," the man said.

"No, Major, nothing much," Traynor replied. He sat back down. "What can I do for you, and excuse me for sitting, but this has been a hectic day."

"Major Marcus DeGaulle, Space Service Medical Corps, Doctor," the man said. "My new assignment is *Polaris*, sir. I found out through the ship's grapevine that you're the new commander of *Polaris*, and felt I should come and introduce myself."

"Good to meet you, Major," Traynor said, extending his hand but remaining seated. DeGaulle stepped forward and shook it. "Have a seat."

"Thank you, sir," DeGaulle said. "And sir, it's Marc. I've never gotten used to being called major. I'm just a doctor, not a military man. I prescribe pills and cure your ills." Traynor smiled.

"OK, Marc. And it's Alex."

Traynor picked up the second folder on the table. It was by far the fullest of the pile. The title of the report was as long as the folder was thick. PERSONNEL STATUS—VETERAN AND INCOMING PSYCHOLOGICAL/PHYSICAL PROFILES—USRFC POLARIS.

"You've got a PS file," DeGaulle said. "Good. I wasn't sure they'd provide you with one. Let me get mine out." For the first time since DeGaulle had arrived, Traynor noticed the large folder under his arm. From the folder, De Gaulle removed a file identical to the one Traynor was holding.

"You do realize there may be a problem with the new personnel?" De Gaulle asked.

"No," Traynor replied. "I haven't been able to get to the PS file yet. I just got my orders today."

"I've had a chance to glance through the data sheets," De Gaulle told Traynor. "Not the personal sheets, mind you. But from going over the data sheets, one major problem seems to be the number of new personnel. Over two hundred and fifty."

"Two hundred and fifty?"

"That's right. Two-fifty-nine, to be exact," De Gaulle replied, finding the figure on the sheet of paper before him.

"What the hell did Hawkins do to that ship?" Traynor asked angrily, of no one in particular.

De Gaulle paused for a moment, letting Traynor's anger cool, then continued.

"Officers of command rank. Excluding yourself," De Gaulle said. "Colonel Carl Nelson. Forty-one. Earther. Veteran of *Polaris*."

Traynor glanced over his copy of the profile De Gaulle was reading from. The sheet described a hot-headed, opinionated stickler for regulations.

"Sounds like a regular smartass," Traynor said.

"I understand he is," De Gaulle replied. "When Captain Hawkins was transferred on arrival at Orbital Station Fifteen, Nelson expected to be bumped up to captain and given *Polaris*."

"Could be the impetus of a big problem," Traynor decided.

"Even more so," De Gaulle continued. "It could blossom into a problem involving politics. Many of *Polaris's* remaining personnel are Earthers, with a number of them belonging to the Earth First party. From what I understand, Hawkins was the leader on the *Polaris*, and since he's gone, Nelson steps into the slot."

"I see," Traynor said thoughtfully.

"Next, we have Colonel Danart N'goto. Science officer. Forty. Earther. Completely qualified, reasonably high marks at the academy, but there are recommendations that he is not psychologically capable of commanding. Is a follower, not a leader," De Gaulle said.

"Wonderful," Traynor commented sarcastically. "Next?"

"Last officer at command rank is the Chief Engineer, Colonel Vladimir Corensky. Forty-six. Earther. Service experience twenty-eight years," De Gaulle read from the file. "Capable, though not one of the best. His file shows several problems that might arise. His psychological profile, broken down to laymen's terms, indicates an inflated image of himself, coupled with a very deep-seated inferiority complex."

"I was under the impression that egomania and inferiority complexes were on the opposite end of the spectrum when dealing with human personalities," Traynor said, his interest aroused.

"Well. . . .yes and no," De Gaulle replied slowly. He sat thoughtfully for a moment. Then he continued. "The best way to explain it is by using the conscious and subconscious. Consciously, Corensky believes himself to be the greatest engineer in the history of mankind. Of course, I'm exaggerating somewhat to make the point clearer."

"Of course," Traynor smiled.

"Subconsciously, however, Corensky knows he is not as good an engineer as he believes. The result: conflict within the individual which may be manifested, as indicated on his chart, by abusive treatment of subordinates, displays of uncontrollable emotion, and physical violence."

"And they let him run loose?" Traynor gasped. "He should be in a mental facility."

"Perhaps I allowed my enthusiasm to run away with me," De Gaulle apologized. "On record, there are no attributable acts of violence, and only a few reprimands for abuse of subordinates. That doesn't mean there haven't been any. Corensky and Hawkins were close. The Captain would hardly put a friend on report unless there was no way of avoiding it. Especially if the Captain held the same ideals."

"Politics again," Traynor sighed disgustedly. "Don't people know there's a war on?"

"War and political intrigue seem to run hand in hand," De Gaulle replied simply.

"I see. You're a philosopher as well as a doctor," Traynor laughed.

"Among my many talents," De Gaulle replied, echoing the laugh.

Then they returned to the files, and spent the rest of the night discussing the personnel of the *Polaris*.

II

The landing craft opened its hatch as soon as it was within the hangar deck of the USR *Polaris*. Three Fleet colonels, wearing dress whites, stood waiting while the hatch opened. At the entrance stood the new captain of the *Polaris*, Alexander Traynor.

Colonel Carl Nelson, acting commander of the *Polaris*, sized up the newcomer. Medium height, fair skinned, fair haired, a hard set to his jaw.

The hangar deck of the *Polaris* measured one hundred twenty-five meters long and one hundred meters wide. In actuality, the hangar deck took up several levels. Within the huge hold rested the fifteen landing craft—the only mode of transportation from the ship to a planet's surface.

Launching and receiving the small ships had been ingeniously devised to allow the hangar deck to remain pressurized at all times. Each landing craft, when fully operational and at its assigned position in the hangar, rested on panels that were actually large elevators to lower the craft. When the craft was completely prepared for launch, the elevator lowered it some six meters. Panels slid into place above the craft and the area was depressurized. The lower panels slid away, and a pressor beam in the upper panels pushed the ship out of its pressure chamber. When it was safely away from the mother ship, the landing craft activated its engines.

Returning to the mother ship was a simple matter of reversing launch procedure. The smaller ship maneuvered until a secondary tractor beam, located alongside the pressor beam in the landing craft's pressure chamber, caught hold of the smaller ship.

Nelson stepped forward, came to attention, and saluted.

"Good to have you aboard, Captain," Nelson said. Traynor returned the salute.

"Good to finally be aboard, Colonel," Traynor replied. "You will have someone bring my things to my cabin?"

"Aye sir."

Marcus De Gaulle stepped out of the small ship and saluted Nelson.

"Major Marcus De Gaulle reporting, sir."

"Ah, yes, Major," Nelson replied, returning the salute.

"Now that we have that settled, let's get down to business," Traynor said gruffly. "I want all department heads in conference room 'A' in thirty minutes. Tell them to come prepared to answer all my questions."

"Sir, I wanted to introduce. . ." Nelson started to say, but Traynor cut him off.

"I'll meet everybody at the briefing. Now move!"

Taken aback somewhat, Nelson turned on his heel and hustled off. The two colonels waiting at attention fell into step behind him.

"Was that a wise move, Alex?" De Gaulle asked. "Getting him angry this early."

"Sure makes things interesting," Traynor replied, his mouth spread in a wide grin. "Shall we go?" Two young lieutenants picked up the bags of the captain and chief surgeon and followed the officers. The heavier belongings would be moved later.

Thirty minutes to the second after the order had

been given, *Polaris*'s new captain sat at the head of a large table in conference room "A." Ten faces confronted him. Two people at the table, Carl Nelson and Marcus De Gaulle, Traynor had met. The others were strangers to him by sight, though two of the older men Traynor recognized as having been on the hangar deck when he boarded. Traynor knew each one, though, from pictures and descriptions in the PS file.

At his right hand was the executive officer, Carl Nelson. Mentally Traynor went over his chart. Stickler for regulations, the chart said. Well, that seemed evident. Nelson sat in the only seat that was reserved when the captain of a USR vessel called a briefing: first chair, right side. It was an old regulation, dating from the first interplanetary flights. Supposedly, it was a result of the belief that the exec was the captain's right-hand man. Most often, at least on the ships Traynor had served on, the participants at a briefing sat where they could find a seat.

On Nelson's right sat one of the two human females. Victoria Spencer, Traynor's brain clicked out. Navigation. Thirty-nine. Still a good-looking woman, though not an exceptional beauty. The set of her jaw indicated the hard core within.

Next sat Major Ben Peters, chief pilot. Blond, fair, a very open face hiding a very closed, introverted personality. How he had risen as high as he did was a mystery to Traynor.

Science Officer Danart N'goto was next. A very dark-skinned Negro. Ivory teeth showing in a sickly sweet smile. What was it the PS file said? Not fit for command.

The last Earther was the one Traynor was most interested in. Vladimir Corensky. A huge, hulking man, well over one hundred ninety-five centimeters, and an easy one hundred fifteen kilos. He sat broodingly, staring at his clasped hands on the table. If there was to be any violence aboard *Polaris*, Traynor knew Corensky would be at the center.

Opposite the Earthers sat the outworlders. To Traynor's immediate left sat Marcus De Gaulle, chief medical officer. De Gaulle was the only person in the room smiling. In the time Traynor had known the Europan, the captain had never seemed to be able to catch the doctor without a smile on his face.

A large blond fellow sat in the next seat. Traynor identified him as Commander Dron Svenson, weapons officer. Svenson came from Jupiter's moon, Ganymede, the only other inhabited body in the home solar system where the people did not live in enclosed structures. Ganymede was a harsh world, cold and barren. However, the first colonists, and the majority that followed, were from Scandinavian countries, where they experienced a climate similar to what was found on their new home. Svenson was an example of the typical Ganymedan. Standing just over two hundred centimeters, broad shouldered and barrel chested, Svenson's blond hair and fair skin added to the image of the modern-day Viking Ganymedans so often cultivated. His description in the PS file indicated a capable and efficient officer, in the eyes of his academy supervisor.

The second woman in the conference room was seated to Svenson's left. She checked her chronometer from time to time, impatiently. She gave Traynor the impression of an active woman, confined without just cause. The fiery red hair that framed her face and ended at shoulder length, identified her as a native of Io, the moon of Jupiter that had been settled by Scotch-Irish pioneers. She was Myra Shanesey, twenty-six, commander, and the landing craft supervisor aboard *Polaris*.

Mark Carter occupied the next chair. Tall and thin, over one hundred eighty-five centimeters tall while weighing seventy kilos, Carter was a native of Oberon, one of the most interesting planetoids holding membership in the USR.

When World War III had ended, the professional soldiers from the different armies had banded together to colonize one of the few deserted areas left on Earth, the outback of Australia. There, these soldiers raised their descendants to be soldiers above all else. When the colonization of the solar system began, these descendants of the World War III veterans colonized Oberon, a moon of Uranus. On Oberon had grown a society based on the techniques of war, both personal and political. By and large, the finest military minds came from Oberon. As soldiers, the Oberonites were superior to all others save the Ganymedans and the Vendrans, whose constant battle against two point six-five G's allowed the Vendrans to operate with twice the strength and speed of normal humans in one Earth gravity.

Mark Carter was the security officer of the *Polaris*. A quiet man, he went about his business with the calm assurance of an Oberonite. He was a commander, twenty-nine, with ten years of experience.

The last member of the conference was the only alien creature at the meeting. Major Kran was a female Pronethan, and the head of the communications department.

Pronetha was the only planet of the Barnard System found to be inhabited when the USR first explored space. Pronethans were a race of creatures that were not quite human, and yet, more than human in many aspects. They were short of stature, broad-shouldered, with no eyes. They used ultrasonic sonar to maneuver about, and were telepaths to the extent that they could read minds unless the person they were interested in was consciously blocking the Pronethan's probing thoughts.

"Good day, ladies and gentlemen," Traynor began. "I'm sure by now everyone knows that I am the new captain of *Polaris*. My name is Alexander Traynor. I'd present my record for you to view, but I feel that we can dispense with that and get on to the important business at hand—namely, getting *Polaris* battle-ready!" Traynor let that sink in before he continued. "I'm ready to hear the section reports." He turned his head to Carl Nelson expectantly.

Nelson glanced at the notes before him.

"Personnelwise," Nelson began, "we are at ninety-five percent of full complement. Three hundred fifty-seven members of the crew are on board at this time. Of the crew members not on board, fifteen are in transit from Sol system, two in transit from Sirius system, and one is an Orbital Station Nineteen, orbiting Vendra, awaiting transportation to this station.

"The missing people represent the following: six security specialists, two lab technicians, three navigation specialists, three medical techs, three communications specialists, and one nurse.

"Life support is now capable of handling a full crew."

"Thank you, Mr. Nelson," Traynor said.

"There's more sir," Nelson said.

"Submit it in written form at the end of the meeting. Sciences?"

"Colonel Danart N'goto sir, science officer," the black said.

"Proceed."

"The central computer system has been replaced. The new system is operational and waiting to be programmed. Everything else is contingent on the programming of the computer. I have one of my best men on it,'' N'goto explained.

''Marshall?'' Traynor asked. N'goto exchanged swift glances with Nelson.

''No, sir. Dickson,'' he answered slowly.

''What do you have Marshall doing?''

''The laboratories on the lower decks are being completely refitted,'' N'goto answered. ''Marshall is supervising the work.'' He paused for a moment. ''Dickson is quite capable,'' N'goto added, stressing the sentence to pass on, subtly, that Dickson was an Earther.

''I see,'' Traynor said thoughtfully. ''Dickson must be quite capable, especially since the man he is superior to is the man who designed the K-96 computer, standard computer for all USR ships of light cruiser status or higher.'' A look of surprise crossed the black's face. ''Oh, yes,'' Traynor continued. ''I keep abreast of these things. It might do you wise, Colonel, to be more aware of these things. Mr. N'goto, Major Marshall knows more about that computer than anyone else in the Republic. Put him on the programming problem. Immediately!'' His voice was soft; but carried with the air of command.

''Aye, sir,'' N'goto said slowly. ''I just thought. . .''

''Well don't!'' Traynor snapped. ''I take it you have nothing else to report until the programming sequence has been completed?''

''Aye, sir.''

''Medical?''

''I'll need more time, Captain, having just arrived myself,'' De Gaulle grinned.

''Get me the report as soon as possible,'' Traynor replied. ''Navigation?''

''Spencer, Major, chief navigator,'' Spencer spoke up. ''Being without computers has been our major problem.''

''It's been the major problem of the entire ship, Major,'' Traynor remarked.

''That's true, sir, but with Colonel Nelson's help, the navigation section has been able to work up a majority of its navigational tapes and programs. Colonel Nelson arranged for Station Fifteen to let us use the big computers during off hours; third shift and early first shift. We're able to get sometimes three and four hours of computer time on a trip to the station.''

''Very good, Major,'' Traynor said agreeably. ''Very resourceful of you and the Colonel. How prepared are you?''

''We have all the routine tapes in the can, sir, but the more complicated programs take longer than we've had at the computers,'' Spencer explained. ''A couple of the programs need three or four people working at the computer for six to eight hours.''

Traynor turned to his executive officer.

''Nelson, when this is over, get on the line to the station. Use my name and get hold of Admiral Antonozzi. Make an official request for the use of a computer bank for a twenty-four-hour period, preferably immediately.'' Traynor turned back to the navigator. ''Spencer, when it comes through, which I'm sure it will, get your entire section over there and get your programs run. You can have your programs prepared for Marshall to put into the computer.'' Traynor checked the papers Nelson had set before him.

''You're short three specialists. Take three security men to fill in. Carter can help you find three with some experience in navigation.'' Carter nodded.

''Thank you, sir,'' Spencer replied.

''Security?''

''Seventy-nine security personnel on board sir,'' Mark Carter said. ''Most are on their first mission.''

"I want a breakdown of security. Age, home planet, years in service, rank graduated from academy. I already have files on each, but I want a list."

"Aye, sir," Carter agreed. "I have a breakdown with me. I'll have a copy made."

"Vendrans, Ganymedans, and Oberonites in security?"

"Twenty, twenty-five, and twelve," Carter answered.

"Excellent." Traynor smiled. "Thank you, Commander. Weapons?"

"The new weapon systems are being installed now," Svenson began. "Primary tractor and pressor beams are set. Secondaries are fine. The heavy deflectors are operational when power is restored. Matter deflectors are still down. I have two men on them now."

"Carter, let Svenson have any men you can dig up with some experience in weapon systems," Traynor commanded.

"At least four or five, Dron," Carter stated.

"I'd appreciate it," Svenson said gratefully. "We've been primarily concentrating on the matter deflectors and the laser cannon. We've had no time to work on the disruptors. The parts for the systems are waiting at the station for someone to pick them up, but I haven't had time to get them."

"Carter, I hate to keep taking men away from you, but security is the best source of manpower," Traynor explained. "We'll need two crews to shuttle those parts over here. If I'm any judge of weapons, those crates will be enormous. Probably want all-Vendran crews. Eight men should do it. You go along as receiving officer."

"Aye, sir," Carter acknowledged the assignment.

"Sir, don't you think I ought to be the receiving officer?" Nelson asked.

"We have a ship to put together, Mr. Nelson,"

Traynor said. "I won't send any of my command officers anywhere while this craft is non-operational! Besides, these crews will be security men. It's a good chance for some morale boosting. Maybe if we get started, we might turn the morale of this ship around soon."

"Aye, sir," Nelson said softly.

"Good," Traynor agreed. "Svenson, how about the High-Energy Heat Beam?"

"Fleet specialists have been installing it for the past week," Svenson replied. "I was told that when installation was completed, the man in charge would provide the Captain with the proper firing-sequence procedure."

"Where is the projector located on the hull?"

"Between the foreward laser banks," Svenson replied.

"Thank you. Communications?"

"We are operating with relatively new personnel, sir," the Pronethan began. "And also, as was reported earlier, Communications is without three people.

"Our equipment has been installed. We are waiting for the computer to be prepared that we may discover whether our equipment is operational. The department members have been on shifts, familiarizing themselves with the equipment thoroughly, while monitoring the one communication link we have functioning; the link with Station Fifteen."

"Very good Major Kran," Traynor complimented the creature. "Have you run into any serious problems?"

"No, sir," Kran replied.

"Very good, Major. Pilots?"

"Well, uh, sir, we have no real problems," Peters began. "We, uh, can't test, uh, our equipment until we have, uh, full power. Other than that, we have our equipment installed, and, uh, I'm having the, uh, n-new personnel g-go over the equipment to l-learn it."

"OK, Peters," Traynor said softly. "Commander Shanesey, tell me about the little birds."

"As ye know, sir," Shanesey's thick accent filled the conference room. "A cruiser this size carries fifteen transports. Of the fifteen on board now, nine are new, and two of the old birds need engine repair. I can only certify five ready for flight."

"You said we received nine new birds but only five are flyable?" Traynor questioned. "Did we receive four non-operational transports?"

"I've only certified one of the new transports," Shanesey explained. Seeing Traynor's questioning look, she continued. "Only transports I've checked over myself are certified flyable on this ship. If ye want to change that policy, ye'll have to get rid of me."

"There'll be no need for that, Commander," Traynor replied smiling. "However, leave the two down for engine work alone until you've got the other birds ready."

"Very good, sir," she answered. Under her breath, she continued: "It was what I'd intended to do." Though it was spoken softly, Traynor's ears caught Shanesey's last remark. He glanced over at her from where he was standing, winked, and smiled. Shanesey caught his eye, realized he had overheard her remark, and blushed as red as her hair.

"Engineering?"

Corensky looked up from the papers he had been involved with.

"Sir?" he asked questioningly.

"Your report, Colonel, please," Traynor explained.

"Ah, yes, my report," Corensky replied slowly. "Our neutronium pile has been successfully installed within its shielded walls. We should soon have the neutronium drive operational.

"As for our sub-light engines; we have been having some trouble getting them set. Major LeMay was supposed to have them operational by now. She doesn't seem to have them working yet. If and when she has them set, *Polaris* will have nearly full power. Right now we're operating on power from Station Fifteen. We have a radio-energy hook up."

"Are you having any personnel problems, Colonel?"

"Only Major LeMay," Corensky said flatly. "She's had almost two weeks to get the sub-light engines operational. She doesn't seem to be able to handle it. I've been planning on taking over the job myself, but haven't got around to it yet."

"I'll check into the problem myself," Traynor cut him off. "Submit anything else in writing. And that will be all, ladies and gentlemen." They rose and filed out, leaving Traynor and De Gaulle alone.

"That was interesting," De Gaulle broke the silence. "From some of the looks you were getting, Alex, I'd say you were not welcome."

"Unfortunately, Marc, I think you're right," Traynor answered thoughtfully.

Replacing the disruptors of a Fleet heavy cruiser can be one of the most difficult and demanding jobs of a weapons officer. Heavy cruisers sport the largest, most powerful, and most sophisticated disruptor systems known to the Fleet.

Replacing the disruptors of the *Polaris* required three steps. Step one, receiving the equipment. Not always the easiest step, as Dron Svenson was finding out. Two security details of eight men each, along with Mark

Carter, were transported in two of the larger landing craft to Orbital Station Fifteen. Each crew was assigned to load one large disruptor housing, boxed and ready for shipment, into its respective craft. Smaller boxes containing guidance controls, fire controls, power-amplification generators, and other vital parts, were loaded also.

The two crews Carter had selected had been chosen with care. As expected, the weapons system weighed in the general area of eleven hundred-fifty kilos. Eight normal men, even eight men possessed of greater than normal strength, would have found great difficulty in handling much more than seven hundred-fifty kilos. Yet the men chosen were able to handle the huge weight with ease, for Commander Carter had chosen sixteen of the twenty Vendrans available to him from the security department.

Vendrans are natives of the planet Vendra, the second planet in the Barnard system to be discovered by Earth explorers. Discovered in 2084, it was settled in 2090. Independence was granted in 2115. The Vendran members of *Polaris*'s crew were representative of the sixth generation or native-born Vendrans.

Vendra's planetary size marked it as the largest planet in the three settled solar systems of the USR. Slightly larger than both Jupiter and Alpha Barnard, it was the only member of the big three to possess an atmosphere capable of supporting life. The planet supported six billion people, spread on six of ten major continents. The planetary government actively supported the idea of large family units. Some families included fifteen to twenty children in one household.

The major feature of Vendra that made the inhabitants different from other humans in the USR was the gravitational field of the huge planet. Vendran gravity, at 2.65 Earth gravity, represented the strongest gravitational field of the member planets, though two members of the Sirius system, colony planets, had stronger gravities. Normal humans have great difficulty functioning in Vendra's gravity. The first colonists on Vendra had the same problem of adaptation to the strong gravity: the incessant pulling on the body, the ever-present danger of falling at over two and a half times normal speed. Many of the first colonists died of small accidents.

The colonists were determined to survive, though, and survive they did. Beginning with the first generation of native-born Vendrans, remarkable physical changes began to take place. Their bodies became shorter and broader, with large, broad shoulders. Their hearts increased in size to pump blood through their bodies. Bones became thicker and less easy to break. Cartilage strengthened until it had the toughness of normal bones.

The Vendrans of *Polaris*'s security section, taken as a group, were average Vendrans, standing between one hundred forty-five and one hundred-sixty centimeters. What made them the important members of the crew they were, were their unique abilities when functioning in one Earth gravity. Accustomed to a much stronger pull on their bodies, the Vendrans were able to move with speed and quickness nearly blinding to the eyes of the others aboard *Polaris*. Their muscles, used to countering the immense gravity of Vendra, allowed the Vendrans to be virtually supermen in Earth's gravity.

For that particular reason, Mark Carter had selected the Vendrans as the crews he used to bring aboard the disruptor systems. Eight average Vendrans could move the crates with very little difficulty. Eight Vendrans of the caliber aboard *Polaris* were capable of moving over two thousand kilos with relative ease. Because of the bulkiness of the disruptors, the eight-man crews were necessary to successfully load the huge casings into the transports.

Step two involved transporting the equipment from the hanger deck of the *Polaris* to the weapons section. While it was possible for the security men escorting the disruptors from the station to carry the huge engines of destruction to the weapons section, Dron Svenson was prepared with an easier way to transport the equipment. He waited on the hangar deck with a Z-grav generator.

Z-grav, discovered in 2120 by Clayton Foster of Triton, proved to be the major breakthrough in the neutralization of gravity. Z-grav generators formed field platforms onto which the object of concern was placed. The weight of the object was effectively negated. Z-grav, however, only neutralized the weight, not the mass, of an object. Whereas it required eight Vendrans to move an eleven-hundred-fifty-kilo object effectively, it still required three Vendrans to provide the locomotion and guidance when using Z-grav fields.

The Vendrans lowered the huge casings to the waiting Z-grav fields. At one end of the casings, Dron Svenson activated a force guidance clamp. One man, holding the activator and walking ahead, could guide the cargo field successfully. Two men were required to provide locomotion by pushing the casing and Z-grav platform.

The remaining members of the security detail loaded the smaller units onto other Z-grav platforms. These platforms were moved along to join the larger units.

Under Mark Carter, and Dron Svenson's skillful guidance, the small convoy was successful in negotiating the corridors and passages to the aft-end of deck "G" where, using the cargo lift, one by one the platforms were raised to "A" deck. Svenson held the convoy in the corridor outside the lift until all the units were on the same level. He rechecked his clearance through the captain, then slowly began to guide the men and equipment through interconnecting passages toward the weapons section, some two hundred meters forward.

Navigating the passages of "A" deck required a great deal of ingenuity. More than once, the huge casings wedged themselves immobile when making a turn of more than seventy-five degrees. The men moving the equipment were forced to deactivate the Z-grav field and bodily dislodge the piece, placing it into the next passage before reactivating the Z-grav field.

Finally, after a great deal of sweat and struggle, along with three minor muscle strains, the equipment was successfully tucked into the weapons section.

The weapons section of the *Polaris* consisted of three large rooms on "A" deck and two smaller rooms on "B" deck, plus interconnecting stair wells within the weapons area. One of the large rooms was devoted to the actual mechanisms of the laser banks. The six huge units occupied three quarters of the room, leaving barely enough space for specialists to keep up-to-date checks on the equipment. The second room on the upper level was the home of the disruptor beams, and, since the Fleet specialists had arrived aboard *Polaris*, also where one of the newest Fleet weapons, the High Energy Heat Ray, could be found. It was this second room that Svenson directed the Vendrans to bring the casings. The miscellaneous equipment that had also arrived was divided between the main weapons control room and the power relay controls in the rooms on "B" deck.

Once the equipment had been delivered, step three, actual installation of the equipment, took place.

Traynor moved confidently down the corridor. Two standard days had passed since his first conference with *Polaris*'s department heads. The new captain's confidence was slowly growing as he made his presence felt on the ship. Operations were beginning to run smoothly. All areas of the ship were progressing by leaps and bounds, save one; repair on the sub-light engines. Traynor was on his way to engineering to find out firsthand what the problem was.

Towering over the personnel ahead of him, a blond giant who, Traynor reasoned, could only be a Ganymedan Swede, moved gracefully toward the captain. He wore the insignia of a security specialist and the rank of lieutenant. The giant rose a good head taller than anyone in the corridor, perhaps two hundred-twenty centimeters. Traynor motioned the man over.

"Where you headed, Lieutenant?" Traynor asked.

"Reporting to Commander Carter, sir," the Ganymedan replied.

"You're on me now," Traynor said. "We're headed for engineering. I'll call Carter from there and tell him you're with me."

"Aye, sir," the giant answered, falling into step with the captain. "My name is Nater, sir, Harold Nater. Everyone calls me Hal."

"Well, Hal, tell me what you know about engineering?"

They reached an elevator and Traynor punched the proper sequence of numbers into the console. Nater was silent for a moment.

"Do you want the official report, or the truth?" he asked at last.

"Both."

"Well, I'm sure you know the official report. Colonel Corensky, the supposed force that gets everything done in engineering. He's on top of everything, in command, and when something goes wrong in engineering, he's the man to see," Nater said.

"Isn't that the way it should be?" Traynor interrupted rhetorically.

"Of course, sir," Nater agreed. "But on *Polaris*,

that's a lot of bull."

"What makes it different on *Polaris*?"

"Sir, your being an Earther makes that a difficult question to answer," Nater said evasively.

"Whether I come from Earth, or Vendra, or Titan, or Hell itself doesn't matter! What matters is this ship! Something is tearing it apart internally, Lieutenant, and I want to know what it is!"

"Well, sir," Nater told the captain, "Colonel Corensky is not everything the official report makes him out to be. He doesn't have the push to make everything go, and he's not on top of everything, like the report says. If there's a problem in engineering, and you want to get it solved, the person to see is Major LeMay. She knows more about neutronium-drive engines than almost anyone in the fleet."

"Then what's she doing working on the sub-light engines?"

"That's what I'm coming to sir," Nater replied. "Colonel Corensky is intimidated by her obviously superior knowledge and engineering capability. To cover his inferiority, he pushes the menial tasks off on Major LeMay. Also, he assigns her assistants, which allows him to pick the most disruptive crewmen for her. Of course, they do their very best to give her as many problems as possible.

"Finally, there's Colonel Corensky. Major LeMay feels the brunt of his anger, but everyone in engineering, especially the outworlders, have fallen victim to his temper. He constantly shouts, rants, and raises holy cain over the least little problem. Last week he came down on Major LeMay and Shawn O'Leery, one of the engineers, because a barrel was on the lower deck of the engine room and was supposed to be on the upper deck. They tried to explain that both O'Leery and LeMay had rushed to the aid of a youngster, on his first cruise, who stuck a probe where it shouldn't have been and was sent flying across the room. That only sent Colonel Corensky into more of a rage.

"It didn't help Major LeMay when the Colonel came down on her that hard. He spouted off regulation after regulation, O'Leery told me, and she just went deeper and deeper into her shell. She's an introvert, anyway, and now she barely talks to anyone unless it's unavoidable."

The elevator door opened and they stepped out into a busy corridor. Across the passageway was the entrance to the engine room.

"You seem to be in the know on *Polaris*," Traynor said thoughtfully, as they crossed to the engineering doors.

"When you stand out like I do, sir, you get noticed," Nater replied. "And when you get noticed, you become informed."

The doors to engineering opened on a scene that made Traynor, as captain of the *Polaris*, shudder.

A pretty blonde woman, wearing black work coverals and on the verge of tears, was shouting orders to two men leaning against a huge barrel, laughing. Four others, on the upper level of the engine room, looked on concernedly.

"And I'm not going to order you again! Move that barrel or I'll. . .I'll. . ." and then the tears came.

"Major Erica LeMay," Nater whispered to Traynor. The girl pushed past the two newcomers, not even realizing who they were. A young lieutenant on the upper deck, watching the major leave, caught sight of the braids on Traynor's sleeve.

" 'Ten-hut!" she cried out. All within the two-level engine room, save Traynor and Nater, came to attention. Traynor motioned the young lieutenant, a pretty little Ioan with the telltale red-hair characteristic of the natives of that world, to him.

"Find Major LeMay. Tell her I want her to report to sickbay. Directly to Major De Gaulle. She's to get something to calm herself down and rest. Also, tell her I want a complete written report of this incident. There's no rush, but as soon as she feels up to it. Go!" Traynor then spoke to Nater.

"Send one of the others to sickbay. You pick the proper one, if you get my drift. He's to report directly to Major De Gaulle. Tell De Gaulle what happened and that LeMay is coming. If she isn't there soon, De Gaulle should find her."

Traynor turned to the offenders, a commander and a lieutenant, both at attention. The commander started to speak.

"Shut it!" Traynor growled. Nater, having dispatched a lieutenant to sick bay, stepped over to stand beside Traynor. The huge Ganymedan's face was set in a grim frown, similar to the captain's.

"Lieutenant Nater, please describe, in your own words, the incident you witnessed here," Traynor said. To the two offenders he continued: "This is for my benefit. I am interested in knowing whether Lieutenant Nater witnessed exactly what I did." The lieutenant, a youngster probably no more than twenty-two, paled.

"When I entered the engine, room, Captain," Nater began, stressing the word "captain," "I witnessed a senior officer of the USRFC *Polaris* issue a direct order to two junior officers of that same ship. I witnessed the two previously mentioned junior officers not only disobeying the order, but laughing in their superior's face."

"Thank you, Lieutenant Nater." Traynor nodded to the Ganymedan. "Gentlemen," he began, addressing the two men before him. "That was the most disgusting display of insolence to a superior officer I have ever witnessed!"

"But Captain. . ." the youngster began.

"Lieutenant, for your own good, keep quiet," Nater said softly.

"Because every member of this crew is needed to get this ship into fighting shape, I am not going to bring you up before a military court on the charge of mutiny. However, I am putting both of you on report, which will entail a bit of extra duty. Also, because of your actions when dealing with the Major, I am requiring that you write an apology to Major LeMay, and present it to her personally. You will, of course, bring it to me and I will approve it before it goes to the Major. And," Traynor continued harshly, "If you are ever involved in something like this again, there will be no time wasted on a trial! I'll drop you on Alpha Barnard with one air tank! Is that understood?" Both men knew of the airless world of Alpha Barnard. One air tank would last a man a day.

"Aye, sir!" they answered.

"Get to work!"

"Thank you, sir," the young lieutenant added. His partner turned quickly and began moving the barrel. The grateful youngster turned to help him.

The communication visiscreen beeped. Nater, nearest the console, stepped to it and flipped the switch. He motioned to the captain.

"Major De Gaulle, sir."

"Marc, did you get my message?"

"Got 'em, Alex," De Gaulle answered. His face smiled out from the screen. "LeMay showed up with the lieutenant you sent here. Gave her a tranquilizer and got her to rest in one of the wards. Just called to let you know."

"Good."

"She said she only came down because it was a

direct order from you. She's scared to death you're upset because she left her post while on duty."

"Tell her that she was officially off duty the minute I stepped into engineering, so she didn't desert her post and she shouldn't be worrying her pretty little head about it," Traynor said.

"She is a pretty one," De Gaulle smiled. "Out." Traynor laughed, punching the screen controls to contact security. Mark Carter's face appeared on the screen.

"Just to let you know that Hal Nater's with me and will be for most of his shift."

"Fine by me, sir. Nothing important in the works," Carter replied. "Anything else?"

"Not that I can think of," Traynor responded. "Out."

"Commander." Traynor called to a young woman on the upper deck as he turned from the screen. She came to the top of the connecting stairwell. "You're in charge here. I don't think you'll have any problems. Your lieutenants should be back any time now." Traynor exited the room, followed by the giant security officer. The new captain strode confidently down the corridor.

"Where to now, Captain?" Nater asked, his long legs easily matching the captain's strides.

"Why not sickbay," Traynor replied. He felt good. What could have been a major incident had been avoided, and the word, he knew, would be passed quickly. Soon both sides would know where he stood.

Smiling, Traynor swerved to a nearby elevator port. The automatic doors slid silently open and he stepped in, Nater following. The small computer console accepted his deck coordinates and delivered the two men three doors down from sickbay. They entered the medical section and were greeted in the outer section by a bright young technician.

"De Gaulle still here?" Traynor asked.

"The Major's in his office," the girl replied.

"Which ward is Major LeMay in?"

"Ward 'A', sir," was the answer.

"Hal," Traynor turned to the Ganymedan. "Check on her. Make sure she knows everything's OK, then come on into De Gaulle's office. Don't worry about knocking."

The big fellow nodded and passed through the door marked Ward "A". Traynor knocked on the chief surgeon's door.

"Yo," De Gaulle called from within.

"Just me, Marc," Traynor said, opening the door. "Checking up on you."

"Come on in, Alex," De Gaulle stood behind his desk. Several stacks of papers littered it.

Traynor accepted the proferred seat. De Gaulle plopped back into his chair.

"Just trying to get caught up," he laughed. "It's almost impossible."

"How's it going down here?" Traynor asked, chuckling.

"Terrible," De Gaulle winced. "Papers coming out of my ears. Everytime I get almost caught up, someone brings in another pile."

"I take it you've been busy," Traynor laughed.

"Busy! De Gaulle responded loudly. "Except for LeMay, all I've done is catch up on my predecessor's unfinished business."

"Seriously, though, have you had any problems?"

"Well," De Gaulle answered slowly. "I've only got four or five Earthers under me. They seem to be at the heart of the ship's problem, if you'll excuse me for speaking bluntly about the people of your home. The four techs aren't a factor, but the doctor, Jenkins, is a definite candidate for top pain in sickbay. In my brief contacts with him, I have given him three direct orders, and he questioned all three."

"Handle it?" Traynor asked, concerned.

"Yeah," De Gaulle laughed. "I ignored him. Gave several of the nurses the giggle. Seems Major Jenkins is not well liked down here, even by the other Earthers. Expected to be the new chief surgeon and has been throwing his weight around."

Nater opened the door and entered at that moment.

"Forgot to tell you, Marc," Traynor laughed, seeing De Gaulle's wide eyes. The Chief Surgeon stared at the huge bulk of the blond giant. "I picked up a sidekick. Marc De Gaulle, Harold Nater, security."

"Major," Nater nodded, saluting. De Gaulle grinned, sticking his hand out as he rose.

"Marc, please," he laughed. "God, how tall are you?"

"Two hundred twenty-two point three-six centimeters," Nater replied, shaking the extended hand. "Tallest crewman on *Polaris*. By point three-six centimeters, no less!" He echoed the doctor's laugh. "And it's Hal." De Gaulle motioned him to a seat, where the Ganymedan settled his bulk, somewhat uncomfortably.

"I do have something I want to talk to you about," De Gaulle said, not looking up from the report he had begun working on. He quickly finished and slid the pile of papers to one side.

"OK, shoot," Traynor said.

"LeMay," De Gaulle began. He paused to gather the complete attention of his two listeners. "I don't know what's going on in engineering, but she's on the verge of a nervous breakdown. Her nerves are shot. One more thing to set her off and she'll go over the edge."

"She's in bad shape, then?" Traynor asked.

"Not yet, but on the threshold," he replied. Then

the surgeon grinned fiercely. "She won't go over if this pill-pusher can help it. I know how valuable she is.

"After I sent her to the ward, I went back over her PS file. Her name sounded familiar, and I discovered how important she is to this ship. You'll need her, Alex, to get this baby going."

"Well, you're the doctor," Traynor replied. "I think she's in capable hands."

"What can we laymen do for her?" Nater asked.

"She needs respect," De Gaulle answered. "She has a terrible inferiority complex. And before you say anything, Alex, it's not like the other inferiority complex we discussed."

"You can talk freely in front of Hal, Marc," Traynor said automatically.

"Very well. Hal, this goes no further than we three," De Gaulle stressed. Nater nodded. The doctor continued his comments to the captain. "Corensky's complex is subconsciously self-imposed. Those types, in their extreme cases, need psychiatric care to regain a better self-image.

"LeMay's case is different. Her complex was forced on her by outside entities. Deep down, in her subconscious if you will, she knows she is a fully competent engineer. However, someone, or several someones, have done their best to destroy her self-image.

"The good thing about LeMay's problem is that, even in extreme cases, if caught before the individual goes over the edge, a sensitive and understanding person can bring about a quick recovery, without actual psychiatric aid. Now, is that clear?"

"As mud," Traynor replied. De Gaulle picked up a pile of documents in a mock attempt at throwing them toward Traynor. "Really, doctor," Traynor laughed. "Is this how you carry out all your consultations?"

"I understand what you're saying," Traynor added

quickly. "A little respect," he continued seriously.

"It's like that all over this ship!" the captain slammed his hand on the arm of the chair. "Outworlders tread softly while Earthers walk confidently. Senior officers fear junior officers. My God, those two in engineering laughed in her face! Their direct superior, and they laugh! I should have thrown the book at them."

"I don't believe you'll have any problem with the younger fellow again," Nater quickly interjected. "I talked with one of the other engineers there while you were on the visiscreen. He was pressured by the older fellow."

Traynor nodded, agreeing. "I got that impression," he said, somewhat calmer. "Hal, since you've started talking, why don't we put you on a spot, and let you tell us what you know about our problem."

"Well, sir," Nater began. "I'll start off by saying that several sections do not have any major problems. Communications, security, weapons, and landing craft maintenance. If you notice, there is one common denominator. All are commanded by outworlders.

"The problems lie in the sections commanded by Earthers. Sciences, navigation, engineering, pilots, and, of course, our executive officer. The senior officers are responsible for the major problems, either directly or indirectly. Corensky, Nelson, N'goto, Peters, and Spencer. Our previous captain and chief surgeon made it seven full fledged members of the Earth First party. No matter what an outworlder did, either it was wrong, or one of the senior officers took credit for the action. Major LeMay is an extreme example, but every outworlder has felt the pressure. Some Earthers too. The ones that try to get along with us outworlders."

"OK, I'll buy that," Traynor said quietly. He thought for a moment, then continued. "What can I do to make up for this loss of faith?''

''Today's incident in engineering is a good start,'' Nater answered. ''It'll travel quickly.'' He laughed. ''Loose-lipped lieutenants.''

''Ah yes,'' Traynor laughed. De Gaulle smiled also.

''To be a lieutenant again,'' De Gaulle said. ''No responsibility. Just follow orders.''

''I really believe you were a lieutenant,'' Traynor said sarcastically. ''You were commissioned a major.'' De Gaulle shrugged his shoulders innocently.

''I can dream, can't I?'' he replied.

''By the way, how is Major LeMay?'' Traynor directed to Nater.

''Fine, just fine,'' answered the Ganymedan. ''Said to thank you.''

''Good. Hal, I'm in need of an executive assistant. Basically a gopher. Want it?''

''Why not?'' Nater replied. ''Be a change.''

''Good. Your first job is to set up a new duty roster. Now that almost all the new personnel have checked in, run the names through the computer for a schedule,'' Traynor explained.

''I want certain people placed on certain shifts,'' Traynor added. ''Put LeMay as engineer on my shift. Give her a crew of outworlders. It'll give her some confidence.'' Nater nodded.

''Don't put Corensky on Nelson's shift. Also, separate Spencer and Peters. Peters on Nelson's shift; Spencer on the third. Let's see, rotate command on the dead man's shift among the piliots. N'goto's on my shift.''

''Can do, sir,'' Nater grinned. He rose and headed for the door. ''No problem at all.''

''Get Marshall to help you,'' Traynor added nonetheless. And inform Carter of your new assignment."

"Aye, sir," Nater replied. "Where can I find you?"

"In my cabin," Traynor smiled. "And my name is Alex. Calling me 'sir' makes me seem so old."

Myra Shanesey leaned her chair against the wall and sipped her drink quietly. The room was bustling with activity; people entering and leaving, coming off or going on duty. Everyone in the lounge carefully avoided the red-haired woman in the corner. She wore her don't-bother-me-or-else look.

Occupying her thoughts at the moment was her brief meeting with the new captain of the *Polaris* at the department heads' briefing. In the two days since the brief encounter, this very moment was the first chance she had been able to squeeze in to relax and try to understand the fleeting impressions she had observed at the conference.

"True he's an Earther," she thought, "but he isn't like one of the smug earth officers I've dealt with on *Polaris* before." The captain seemed to understand the outworlders to some extent. He hadn't been harsh or rude. And he cut Nelson off more than once, and virtually reprimanded N'goto. Yet, he seemed to understand Peters's problem.

The young Ioan was brought quickly back to wakefulness by the sound of someone seating themself in the chair next to her. She looked up to see the bright, familiar face of Shawn O'Leery smiling back at her.

"Shawn O'Leery, if ye persist in scarin' me out of me wits, ye'll be knowin' what 'tis like to be treated in the medical section," Myra growled.

Laughing, O'Leery punched the selectometer at the center of the table. His drink floated from the master distributor on a Z-grav coaster. O'Leery removed the glass and the Z-grav field disappeared.

Shawn O'Leery, a loud, brash, young Irish-Ioan, was a veteran of *Polaris*, serving as an engineering officer with the rank of commander for over two standard years. Both he and Myra Shanesey had joined *Polaris* on the same day and, with their mutual origins and associations, had grown close in their time together.

"Sorry, me darlin'," he replied. "But I thought ye'd be wantin' to hear the news floatin' around the engine room." The girl nodded.

"The new captain, Traynor, was in engineering about the time a couple a boys wasna doin' what Erica ordered. Well, this new boy sent Erica to sickbay to rest, and cussed them boys up one side and down the other."

"It's about time, don't ye think?" asked Myra.

" 'Tis true, darlin', and what they deserved!"

The two Ioans sat quietly for a few moments, each with his or her own thoughts. Myra took a sip of her drink and broke the silence.

"I met this new captain."

"What do ye make of 'im?" O'Leery asked, contemplating his half-filled glass before putting it to his lips.

"I was just goin' over it in me mind when you so unceremoniously made your presence known," she replied, smiling softly. "He's different, Shawn. He's not like Captain Hawkins."

"How so?"

"Well, I don't know," she replied slowly. "I can't put me finger on it. He was all business at the meeting, but there was such a difference. So much more open.

"Oh, and there was one incident that happened. I made a comment about one of his orders to me."

"Ye'll never learn," O'Leery shook his head, a half smile playing on his lips.

"Shush, Shawn," Myra reprimanded the engineer.

"Anyway, I said it softly, so's he wouldna hear it. But he does hear it. And ye know what he does? He winks at me!"

"Winks?" O'Leery laughed, disbelieving.

" 'Tis the truth, on me grandmother's grave," she replied quickly. "Now, if old Captain Hawkins had heard half of what I've said to him under me breath, I'd be in the brig for the rest of me natural life. And he just winks. I'll tell you, it caught me by surprise. Dron Svenson told me I turned a beautiful shade of red."

"That is different," O'Leery chuckled. "I would have loved to see that meself.

"Oh, I ran into Hal Nater," O'Leery continued, changing the subject. "The Captain made him an executive assistant."

"Well, la de da," Myra retorted.

A short, stocky creature waddled up to the table.

"And what are you so indignant about today, Myra Shanesey?" the little Pronethan asked, climbing slowly into a seat.

"Vlres, how are ye?" O'Leery roared, slapping the small creature on the back.

"I would be much better if you would cease that unpleasant habit you persistently continue," Vlres replied. "I do not find the pummelling of my back by your open hand very enjoyable."

"Vlres, Shawn, must ye men continue your personal disagreements in the company of others?" Myra scolded the two.

"Ah Myra, we've no real argument, right Vlres?"

"Much as I hate to agree with this barbarian, he is right," Vlres replied. "But what were you two talking about when I came up?" He took a sip from the drink he had brought to the table, a vile smelling concoction that Pronethans consider a delicacy, and stared at the young woman, if one who is without eyes can be said to stare.

"We were discussing the new captain," Myra answered. "He seems like a good sort, but he is an Earther."

"We must remember," Vlres offered. "All Earthers are not like Captain Hawkins and Colonel Nelson."

"The runt makes sense, Myra," O'Leery grinned. "And it's about time."

Carl Nelson sat at his desk. One light, on his desk top, gave the room a wierd feel. Victoria Spencer, blonde and cold, sat silently opoposite him.

It was Nelson that finally broke the silence.

"Damn those admirals! I was to have been given command of *Polaris*! Don recommended me in his reports when he was bumped upstairs! I just don't understand it!" Nelson slammed his fist down on the desk.

"Well, what do we do?" the woman asked. "*Polaris* was to have been one of the first Fleet ships to come under control of the Loyal Earth party."

"I don't know, Victoria," Nelson replied. "This Traynor could be a problem. He's an Earther, but he acts like an outworlder. Already he's become close with the Europan doctor."

"Which reminds me," Spencer broke in. "He's furnished himself with a special assistant while you've been asleep."

"What?!"

"A Ganymedan security specialist," she continued. "You know, the giant one."

"Nater?"

"That's the one," she agreed. "I was down at the main computer when he comes waltzing in. Calls Marshall over, says he's Traynor's new assistant and needs help programming duty rosters into the computer."

"Well, well," Nelson said. He paused in thought for a moment. "Of all the Loyal Earthers on board, he has to pick an outworlder as an aide. Something will have to be done."

"What?"

"I don't know exactly," Nelson replied. "But pass the word. I want to know everything Traynor does. If he does anything even remotely outside regulations, I'll take him before a review board.

"Also, tell any Loyal Earther on LeMay's shift to give her a hard time. We'll attack him through his senior officers. Same goes for sick bay."

"I don't think the new chief surgeon will be intimidated like LeMay," Spencer said. "And it's going to be hard to get to LeMay. Check the new duty tapes."

Nelson punched the computer console and called up the computerized duty sheet. He scanned it briefly, calling up the different section rosters. Then he whistled.

"LeMay has an all-outworld shift!" he exclaimed.

"I was there when they programmed it," Spencer said.

"Well, I'll fix that," Nelson laughed darkly. "Computer. Revised duty roster, engineering section."

"IDENTIFY," the cold metallic voice changed.

"Identify?" Nelson looked up at the woman. She shrugged her shoulders.

"Colonel Carl Nelson, Executive Officer, USR *Polaris*."

"NEGATIVE! NEGATIVE!" the computer sounded, a red light blinking on the console. "COLONEL NELSON NOT ELIGIBLE TO REVISE DUTY ROSTER, PER PROGRAMMING."

"Not eligible?" Nelson fairly screamed.

"Explain!"

"LOCKED PROGRAMMING SEQUENCE." was the computer's answer.

Nelson looked over at Spencer, his eyes blazing.

"Isn't the exec responsible for the duty roster?" she asked.

"It's not in the regs, but normally the exec takes care of it," Nelson replied angrily. He turned back to the computer console. "Who is eligible to revise the duty tapes?"

"LOCK SEQUENCE RETRIEVAL BY TRAYNOR, CAPTAIN, COMMAND USR POLARIS; NATER, LIEUTENANT, SECURITY SPECIALIST, USR POLARIS," the computer sounded out. Nelson slammed his hand in the desk top again.

"Damn!"

"Carl, take it easy," Victoria Spencer said quietly.

"I'm going over there and have a talk with Traynor!" he snarled. He jumped up and headed for the door.

"Is that wise?"

"It may not be, but I'm doing it anyway!"

Traynor was in a heated discussion with the engineering officer on duty, Commander Shawn O'Leary, when the entry buzzer on the computer console sounded. He hit it unconsciously.

O'Leery's face, on the visiscreen, was troubled. Hal Nater, sitting across from Traynor, mirrored the young engineer's concern.

"We were just running a routine check, sir," O'Leery was explaining. "We added the feeder to the neutronium and started the checklist when there was a power surge that blew secondary relays in two places on 'F' deck and three places on 'G' deck."

An angry Carl Nelson stormed into Traynor's quarters during O'Leery's remarks. Nater rose to his full height, coming to attention. However, Traynor continued his conversation, oblivious to the newcomer.

"Has Corensky been informed?"

"First thing, sir," O'Leery's head nodded. "He's down here checking the computer record of the feeder mix process. Wants to see if it was human error." O'Leery added the last line with a trace of indignation.

"While Mr. Corensky has been checking the tapes," the engineer continued, "I sent a couple of techs to fix the burned-out relays."

"Good man," Traynor commended him. O'Leery signed off. Traynor hoped it turned out not to be his fault.

The captain looked up, noticing Nelson for the first time.

"Yes, Mr. Nelson?"

"I'd like to know why you've put a locked programming sequence on the duty tape!" Nelson demanded loudly.

"Ah, yes, the duty tape." Traynor smiled to himself. "Considering the overhaul this ship has been undergoing, I felt you would have more important problems to occupy your interest. After making specific recommendations, I entrusted the job to Lieutenant Nater. And I must say," Traynor added, "he seems to have done a fine job. Do you have any special question about it?"

Something about the quiet, calm way Traynor spoke took the fire out of Nelson. He was still mad, but he could no longer voice his anger.

"Why did you LPS it, sir?" Nelson asked in a calmer voice.

"Why did you try to change it?" Traynor countered.

Nelson stuttered for a second, but was unable to think of an appropriate answer. He excused himself and exited quickly, almost knocking over the young woman standing in the open doorway.

Timidly, Erica LeMay rapped on the door frame. So soft was the tapping that Traynor, who was vigorously sifting through the papers on his desk, failed to hear it. Nater, his trained ears ever alert, glanced quickly to the entrance, looked back at the captain, and coughed. Traynor looked up, caught his eye, and was directed to the entrance. Seeing the woman there, he rose instantly.

"Major LeMay, it's a pleasure to meet you finally," Traynor exclaimed. "Come in, please! You went off duty so quickly that I didn't get a chance to meet you." He motioned her to one of the seats in the room.

"You do know Lieutenant Nater?" Traynor asked as she sat.

"Yes," she replied softly.

Traynor sat and stared at her for several minutes. She held his gaze for a moment, then lowered her eyes to the floor. Silence hung heavily over the threesome.

Traynor liked what he saw. As a woman, Erica LeMay was an excellent specimen. Blonde, green-eyed, standing one hundred sixty-five centimeters, with a definitely feminine figure, curved in the right places, even in the workman's coveralls she habitually wore. Coupled with what he knew about her mental capabilities, Traynor knew this woman was capable of a lot more than she had shown in her work on *Polaris*.

"Major," Traynor began, breaking the silence. "Let's start out square. I know exactly what happened in engineering today. I also know what has been happening in that section for quite a while now. I understand and I want you to know that I can appreciate your position.

"But I want you to understand mine. I know what

your theoretical capabilities are, and that you've never been pushed to your engineering limits. Theoretically you are the best damn engineer on this ship, bar none. Consequently, when I want something done, it'll be you, not Corensky, that I turn to. Also, because you are the top engineer on *Polaris*, you will feel the brunt of my ranting and raving when we have problems. And let me tell you, lady, I do rant and rave.'' He chuckled. She was listening intently to his every word. ''When this happens, and there is no way it is not going to, you can't let it get to you personally. If you do, you'll crack. And, Miss LeMay, I won't have that!

''When I start ranting and raving, fight back! Don't give me any excuses, but don't lie down and play dead! And don't be afraid to let me know if I'm wrong! I'm not perfect!'' He paused. ''But don't let anyone on board know,'' Traynor added quickly, in a softer voice. ''And if I make a nuisance of myself, throw me the hell out of your engine room.'' The trace of a smile twitched at the corners of Major LeMay's mouth.

''And that's an order, Miss,'' Traynor finished. ''Is that clear?''

''Yes, sir,'' she replied, a bit more confidently. ''Thank you, sir.''

''Thank me?'' Traynor gave her a puzzled look. ''For what?''

''Just thank you,'' she answered, smiling.

''Well, it's good to know everyone hasn't forgotten how to smile.'' Traynor looked down at his papers, then back at the woman, still seated. ''Oh. . .dismissed.'' LeMay stood and saluted, then exited the room. Traynor watched her retreating figure until the automatic door cut his view.

''That's a fine woman,'' he said. Nater nodded agreement.

III

The alert buzzer woke Traynor with a start. The intercom console flashed brilliantly as he rushed to it. From the corridor he heard the computer reinforcing the alert buzzer with a verbal call to battle stations.

"What is it?" Traynor demanded, when Nelson's face appeared on the screen.

"Six enemy battlewagons dropped out of neutronium drive right on top of the station," he replied. "The station took one hit before it could get its screens up. We're the only ship still in synchronized orbit, and the station is overextending its shields to protect us."

"I'm on my way!"

"Aye, sir."

Traynor raced to the nearest elevator and commandeered it from two technicians. Twenty seconds later he burst onto the bridge. Nelson rose from the command chair.

"Weapons," Traynor called to Kran. The communications officer quickly contacted the section. Traynor seated himself in the command chair and spoke into the speaker on the arm.

"Svenson, will our shields hold?"

"Aye, sir," the weapons officer responded. "Matter and heavy are in superior condition. They're the only equipment I'm positive of."

"Good." To Kran, "Get hold of Antonozzi. Tell him we can protect ourselves."

Traynor spun to the engineer on the bridge, Chief Engineer Vladimir Corensky.

"Let's move!" the young captain ordered.

"We can't, sir," the big man replied. "Not enough power to activate the sub-light engines, and the neutronium drive is not yet fully operational."

A voice through the engineering console caused Corensky to turn and speak harsh words in return.

"What was that about, Colonel?" Traynor asked quickly.

"Nothing, sir," Corensky answered. "Just an idea that I don't think is feasible."

"The Admiral won't accept our assessment sir," Kran informed the captain. "Says he intends to keep us under their shields."

"Get me engineering!" Traynor snapped. Corensky turned white. Nelson was totally flabergasted.

"Sir, if Colonel Corensky doesn't feel the idea has any merit, why pursue it?" the executive officer asked.

"Engineering," the console sounded.

"Because I'm captain, Colonel," Traynor replied. "Erica, is that you?"

"Aye, sir," she replied.

"What's the idea?"

"I'm not sure it will work, sir," she said.

"Spill it, woman!" Traynor commanded. The members of the bridge crew exchanged glances of amazement.

"There's a power relay on deck 'C', and another on deck 'D.' If we override those two, along with overriding the master relay, there's a good chance the power surge will activate our sub-light engines."

"What would it entail?"

"Manual burnout of the relay's override key," she replied.

"Sir, I don't think . . . " began Corensky.

"Do it!" Traynor commanded.

The faces of the Earthers on the bridge showed looks of total disbelief. The outworlders radiated a feeling of confidence for the new captain. Traynor stepped to the stellar reference tank.

"Are they firing on us yet?" Traynor asked, leaning over the tank. The question was directed toward David Lornton, the weapons specialist on the bridge.

"No, sir," the Vendran replied.

"Peters, prepare to move at sub-light speed. Heading three-forty-two by three-fifteen."

"Sir, that will put us in the middle of the battle," Victoria Spencer said.

"That's right, Major," Traynor replied. "Put everything on the main screen, Major Kran."

The huge visiscreen on the opposite side of the tank from Traynor lit up. Six huge craft, heavy cruisers or battleships, fired bolt after bolt of energy at the shields of the orbital station. Station Fifteen's shields flashed the different colors of the spectrum.

"Station's first shield down," N'goto informed the bridge.

The battle was not one-sided. The station's huge laser batteries fired continuously. Blast after blast from the heavy disruptor beams pounded against the shields of the enemy craft.

"We're moving, sir," came from Peters.

"Activate shields. Lornton, what's available?"

"Forward laser banks, tractors and pressors."

"That's all?"

"Aye, sir."

"It'll have to do."

Traynor carefully watched the actions of the battle.

N'goto informed him that one of the enemy craft had lost two deflector layers. The third was cracked on the side, and the craft was trying to run.

'Lock tractors on it!'' came the command. Four huge beams of force speared the fleeing craft, holding it immobile. Traynor nodded to Lornton, and both forward lasers were fired at the held ship. In a moment the third shield of the enemy craft fell and the lasers struck the ship midway in its main hull. A huge explosion followed, with metal and debris showering for thousands of kilometers around. The matter shields of The *Polaris* functioned perfectly, causing the flung particles to be bounced away from the ship.

''Come to two-ninety-five by sixty,'' Traynor snapped. ''Prepare tractors.'' A battleship turned toward them. Disruptor blasts rocked the ship, but the heavy shields of *The Polaris* were up to the task. Traynor was able to maintain an upright position as the ship rocked. He examined the ship coming toward them. It was similar in design to *Polaris*, but much larger. Two large neutronium drive generators extended from the aft portion of the main hull. An idea formed in Traynor's mind, and he smiled slightly at the thought.

''Lieutenant Lornton, think you can put a tractor on each one of those generators?''

''Aye, sir,'' he replied. ''No problem.''

''What good would pulling the enemy ship toward us do?'' Nelson asked. Traynor ignored the comment.

''When I give the order, lock two tractors on each generator,'' Traynor began. ''And hit their bow with a pressor. NOW!'' The beams licked out, striking the advancing craft with amazing results. The tractors pulled the stern of the battlewagon forward, while the pressor pushed the bow away, causing the enemy craft to spin on a forward axis. The results left the enemy craft facing away and upside down in relation to the USR craft.

"Hit the tail with all the pressors!" Traynor yelled. Lornton was quick to react. The four beams lashed out and joined together at the stern of the battleship. Audible gasps sounded from behind Traynor as the two neutronium-drive generators, still caught in *Polaris*'s tractors, were sheared from the main hull, which was pushed violently away, striking the matter shields of another enemy craft.

"My God in Heaven," Victoria Spencer gasped.

A disruptor beam from the space station struck the crippled craft, ending its fight permanently.

The enemy squadron, reduced by three, as the station's laser batteries had destroyed another ship, made a valiant attempt to run. Two, however, were caught by the station's high energy heat rays and melted into shapeless masses. The third, preparing to jump to neutronium drive, felt the effects of the newest weapon developed by the USR: the electron separator. The enemy craft ceased to exist.

"Admiral Antonozzi calling, sir," Kran reported.

"Put him on the screen, Major," Traynor requested.

In a brief moment, the visiscreen before Traynor changed. Now filling the screen was the face of a man, approaching fifty, with graying temples and ruddy-colored skin.

"Congratulations, Captain, on a successful engagement," the admiral said.

"Thank you, sir." Traynor replied. He made his way around the navigation console back to his chair.

"That was an interesting new application of pressors and tractors. You do have the entire engagement in the computer?" Traynor glanced to the science officer. N'goto nodded affirmation.

"Yes, sir, we do," Traynor told the admiral.

"Good," the Admiral said. "Computer link and

feed the portion of the engagement dealing with the planning and execution of that particular maneuver."

"Aye, sir," Traynor replied. "Anything else?"

"A damage and status report, Captain," Antonozzi answered. Throughout the interview, the admiral's expression had never changed. "Station Fifteen out."

"*Polaris* out." Traynor paused, then hit the computer/recorder button on his chair console. "Major Kran, put me on shipwide."

The sightless Pronethan's hands flew across her communications board. "Shipwide, sir."

"Thank you, Major," Traynor answered. "This is Captain Traynor. Congratulations, ladies and gentlemen, on a job well done. *Polaris* has just completed her first engagement under my command successfully. Everyone is to be commended on their fine job. I would like to add special commendations to Majors Erica LeMay, Benjamin Peters, and Victoria Spencer, Commander Dron Svenson, and Lieutenant David Lornton on the excellent way they carried out their job. Captain out." Traynor turned to his executive officer. Nelson was at his console, listening to Traynor's speech to the crew.

"Mr. Nelson, you have the con until you are relieved, which should be soon," Traynor said, rising. "As soon as you are relieved, get the damage and status reports ready and give them to Nater. He'll bring them by for me to initial." Striding to the elevator, he threw a last remark to the communications officer. "I'll be in my quarters."

"Yes, sir," Kran replied.

The elevator took Traynor to the corridor outside his quarters. He entered to find two men waiting. Hal Nater rose to attention. Marc De Gaulle remained seated, his face all smiles. He held two glasses, filled with a yellowish liquid.

"Finest Drinan brandy available," De Gaule laughed. "Donated, unknowingly of course, by Major Francis Jenkins." Traynor took the proffered glass. He sniffed the liquid, and smiled his appreciation.

"Don't you think he'll miss it?" Traynor asked laughing. "And Hal, who are you trying to impress?" The giant Ganymedan seated himself.

"I'm glad you made him do that. He makes me feel so inadequate." Traynor laughed at De Gaulle's sarcasm. Nater chuckled agreeably.

"You know, Marc," he began. "I'm really sorry you feel inadequate. Perhaps I should tell Major Upshaw."

'Oh, ho, what's this?" Traynor questioned the doctor. "That name sounds familiar."

"She's the head nurse." Nater quickly supplied the information.

"The Collierite?" Nater nodded yes to Traynor's question. The new chief surgeon of *The Polaris* blushed a brilliant red.

"Well," he began, but Traynor cut him off.

"I take it there were no casualties?"

"One man fell down in a lab," De Gaulle answered. "During the disruptor blasts. Wrenched a knee." De Gaulle stopped. He gazed intently into the young captain's face for several moments. Then he spoke.

"What were you doing, Alex? *Polaris* wasn't and isn't ready for action. You went directly against orders, didn't you?"

"We had shields, we had power, and we had offensive firepower. What more could we have asked for?"

"Oh," De Gaulle's manner changed. "I knew we were moving, but I thought it was because of the blasting we were taking. I didn't know we were at full power."

"We're not," Traynor laughed. "And if Corensky had his way, we wouldn't have any power yet. Erica LeMay came up with a scheme to give us power in the sub-light engines." He drank the brandy and set the glass on his desk.

"I'll tell you, gentlemen, I feel exceptionally good," Traynor sighed. He stretched broadly in his chair. "Nothing could upset me now."

"May I suggest, Alex, that you might be a little more careful when you go against a direct order," Nater interjected. "The word is out. Colonel Nelson wants this ship."

"Expect that," Traynor replied. "You do have a way of depressing people when they least expect it." He smiled grimly. "Where did you hear this?"

"It's floating around," Nater replied solemnly.

De Gaulle had been an interested spectator. Now he stood and crossed over to refill Traynor's glass.

"You must realize Nelson's going to be a constant problem?" the surgeon began. "So why don't you ask for his transfer?" De Gaulle, finished, crossed to the opposite wall and leaned against a protruding chest.

"What reason do I give?" Traynor replied calmly to the doctor's question. The captain, with great difficulty, was maintaining a cool exterior against the conflicting emotions he was feeling. "He's done nothing wrong yet. What do I put on the papers? That he's an Earther? So am I."

"Alex, I think I can understand what Marc is saying," Nater interrupted. He paused to gather his thoughts. "Your major problems are your senior officers. Nelson plans to run a three-three-one on you if he gets a chance. Or maybe a six-three-one."

"Gross negligence?" Traynor was astounded. "Dereliction of duty? On what basis?"

"He has none yet. I hope you won't give him any,"

Nater answered. "But you have given him fuel for a three-four-one."

"A what?" De Gaulle asked from across the room.

"Direct disobedience of a superior officer," Nater quickly informed the doctor. "It's all over the ship."

"How could it be?" Traynor asked. "It just happened a few minutes ago."

"Kran's conversation with the Admiral somehow went shipwide," Nater replied. "I'm sure it wasn't intentional. Anyway, when we started moving, everyone assumed you'd disobeyed orders."

"I see," Traynor answered. "No, I'm sure it wasn't intentional on Major Kran's part. Tell her to check her equipment." He sat back in his chair thoughtfully. The two in the office respected the quiet, remaining silent. De Gaulle stepped to the desk as if to pour himself another drink, thought better of the move, and returned to where he was standing, his empty glass remaining on the desk.

"I see by your status sheets that you have operations well toward completion," Rear Admiral Emilio Antonozzi said, glancing at the papers before him.

"Everything works," Alex Traynor replied. "But I could use another week to get things in top shape."

Traynor was aboard Orbital Station Fifteen, orbiting the planet Mimnon, at the request of the station commander. Traynor had been escorted to Admiral Antonozzi's office. Traynor had been informed that the purpose of the briefing was to present the captain with new orders for *Polaris*.

Antonozzi studied the young captain before him. Reports the admiral had read indicated an intelligent and capable young man. "Still," Antonozzi thought, "he's not much more than a boy. To entrust a Fleet heavy cruiser in the hands of one so young, whether capable or not, is a questionable precedent."

"You've had over a week, not including the time lost because of the enemy attack," Antonozzi reminded *Polaris*'s captain. "Surely you're ready for duty."

"There are still some minor mechanical problems, along with an occasional problem in morale." Traynor winced, expecting a reprimand. Antonozzi's expression did not change.

"I can fully sympathize with your problem," Antonozzi said slowly. "But you must realize that you are not the only one.

"However, your orders have come through. *Polaris* is back to full duty status, as of this moment. You are to proceed to Kappa Barnard to realize *Arcturus* of planet guard."

"Kappa Barnard. That's the mining colony planet."

"Correct," Antonozzi replied quickly. "We have a sub-fleet stationed there because of the importance of the raw neutronium mined from the three drill sites on the planet.

"Captain, what do you know of Kappa Barnard?"

"Basically, that it's a neutronium mining colony," Traynor recited from memory what he had learned at the Fleet Academy more than ten years earlier. "Tenth planet to be discovered in the Barnard system: discovery 2183. Eighth planet out from the star."

Antonozzi hit a switch on the computer console at his desk. The lights, except a small lamp at the admiral's desk, dimmed to blackness. The room became a tank representation of the Barnard system. The holographic image of the tank lit the room to some degree, glowing in its varying colors.

One large white light represented the star. Fourteen lights ranged out from the star. Two, the nearest and the furthest, were a bright blue in color. Blue, Traynor remembered, represented airless planets. One light was green. Green meant planets with atmosphere non-conducive to human development. Poisonous gas for air.

Eleven red lights shown brightly. Eleven planets with Earth-type atmosphere. Eleven inhabited planets developing toward planet-wide independence. Or already independent, with seats on the Interplanetary Council, in the case of five members of the Barnard system.

The green light, eighth from the star, was the one that Traynor and Antonozzi were concerned with.

"Thought this little representation would jog your memory a bit more, Captain," Antonozzi remarked.

"Atmosphere methane gas," Traynor quickly interjected, sufficiently chastised.

"It would do you good to remember that," Antonozzi continued. "Kappa Barnard. Or as the miners call it, the 'Rock.' Just over fourteen thousand kilometer diameter. Gravity: point six-three of Earth. Revolution: five hundred twelve days Earth. Rotation: twenty-nine hours Earth. Three enclosed mining colonies." The admiral finished reverently. Traynor listened patiently, though not with any interest. All the information the admiral had recited could be found in any computer bank.

"You'll be joining a large sub-fleet," Antonozzi continued after a moment. "Besides yourself, there will be nine other heavy cruisers, fifteen light cruisers, and five battleships: *Vera Cruz*, *Golan Heights*, *Normandy Beach*, *Pearl Harbor*, and *Niagara Falls*. And quite a few destroyers and scouts."

"That is quite a big sub-fleet," Traynor commented. The admiral nodded.

"The Rock is the most important planet in this, or any other system. The enemy would do anything to get hold of that piece of real estate, or just destroy it. As long as we have that planet, we can build a fleet of any size. Neutronium is our strength, and the Rock is our best source, now that Jupiter V is mined out."

Antonozzi brought the lights back to normal. He stood, and Traynor did likewise.

"You have your orders, Captain Traynor. When you reach Kappa Barnard space, contact Admiral Willoby aboard *Pearl Harbor*. And good luck!" The admiral saluted. Traynor returned the salute and left the office. Once in the corridor, he brought out his miniature communicator.

"*Polaris* from Traynor." He spoke into the box, leaning against a wall, trying to look inconspicious. Several members of the station's personnel, passing in the corridor, noticed him standing there. Noting his rank, they saluted. Traynor returned the salute.

"*Polaris*, Goldman here," came from the box. "Go ahead, sir."

"Goldman, put me through to engineering." Traynor spoke with authority.

"Engineering," came a feminine voice that was easily recognizable. "LeMay."

"Erica, how soon can we have full power in both sub-light and neutronium drive?" Traynor asked.

"We just finished final checkouts on both." Her voice sounded confident. Traynor had only seen her twice since the audience in his quarters, and had not had a chance to speak with her since the brief enemy attack of two days before. She was becoming more and more confident, and Traynor knew that his backing her against Corensky when the enemy ships first attacked had been extremely instrumental in building up her new-found confidence. "I'd say thirty minutes," she finished.

"I'll be on board in twenty-five. Think you can be

ready by then?''

''Done,'' she answered. Traynor could almost see her smile at his challenge.

''Goldman, still there?''

''Aye, sir,'' came the crisp reply.

''Who's on navigation?'' the Captain asked. ''McMasters?''

''Aye, sir,'' Maria McMasters's soft voice answered.

''Plot a course for Kappa Barnard. Goldman, implement when the little bird is safely tucked. You have the con, Commander.''

''Aye, sir,'' Goldman answered briskly. McMasters echoed him.

''Excellent. Traynor out.'' He returned the communicator to his belt and began to make his way to hangar deck two, where Angela Martin, his pilot, waited to return him to his ship.

'' . . . and so you can see what Traynor has done to our effort,'' Nelson told the others gathered in his quarters. Beside himself in the office were Corensky, Francis Jenkins from sickbay, Reg Dickson of sciences, N'goto, and Peters. All six men were Earthers, all were members of the Earth First party, and all were high ranking members of that same party on *Polaris*. Missing was Victoria Spencer, who was on duty.

''What must be done,'' N'goto told the group. ''Is to disrupt the peaceful existence of this ship as much as possible. Cause internal problems which, coupled with the mistakes our new captain is sure to make, will be enough to bring Traynor before a review board. Even if he doesn't get busted, the fact that his officers brought him up before a board will be enough so that either he'll transfer or the board will transfer him.''

''A good idea,'' came from Francis Jenkins. ''But

how will we do this?''

''Step one: cause problems among off-duty personnel. Step two: problems with on-duty personnel. Three: Traynor has a fondness for outworlders. If we can turn the outworlders against him, we'll be in good shape. Step four: get the Ganymedan out and a loyal Earther in as Traynor's special assistant. Then we can keep an eye on the Captain and catch his mistakes.'' This all came from Nelson, who projected a feeling of great joy in his voice. The others nodded in agreement.

The Vendrans near the entrance to the gymnasium were extremely surprised when their captain entered. He was dressed in a red-and-gray sweatsuit, similar to the outfits the Vendrans themselves wore. He moved slowly, and with great care, accustoming himself to the heavy gravity of the room. The gravity of the room was set to Vendran standard, 2.65 Earth. By the time the captain had moved across the room to a speed bag, the fifteen or so Vendrans had been alerted.

In the days that *Polaris* had been circling the ''Rock,'' rumors had been spreading about the captain. From unknown sources had come quotes attributed to the captain, saying, in effect, that Vendrans were all brawn and no brain; that they were the cannon fodder of the USR, and other similar thoughts. Because of those quotes, the last place a Vendran expected to find the captain was the gymnasium set aside for the Bendrans' special needs.

The captain began to work out with the speed bag. His body and arms worked slowly, fighting the heavy gravity. The men watched him, neglecting their own activities. Slowly the captain became aware of the stares he was receiving. He turned and faced the men. They returned his gaze. One stepped boldly foreward.

''Sir, I'm Peter Trout, security specialist,'' the man

said. He was a typical Vendran, approximately one hundred fifty-five centimeters tall, perhaps ninety kilos, in Earth gravity. Arms fully as large as Traynor's legs. Legs with the circumference some small trees would be jealous of. "I thought perhaps you would like to go a few rounds in the ring." He motioned to one side, where a boxing ring stood. The two men within the ring moved out quickly, removing their gloves.

The captain studied the face of the young man before him. Then he examined the faces of the others within the room. Each expected him to decline the offer, Trout foremost in that opinion.

"Of course, Lieutenant," the captain replied. He moved slowly across the room to the ring. Carefully, he climbed through the ropes. Amazed at his good fortune, Trout hurried to the other side of the ring and entered. Seconds slid gloves on the fists of the contestants.

"Three rounds, three minutes each," the captain called over to his opponent. Trout nodded agreement.

A bell sounded to begin the round. Trout moved quickly out. The captain moved much slower. Trout threw the first blow, a left hook aimed at the captain's chin. Traynor was able to block the blow partially with his shoulder, which moved much slower in the heavy gravity. The blow glanced across the captain's face. Trout followed with a right to the body which doubled the captain up. Two straight lefts were blocked by Traynor's gloves, only because he was covering up. Trout stepped back and swung a left-right combination to the body, followed by two left hooks to the head. Down went the captain. He was up quickly, and during the mandatory eight count, checked himself for any serious injuries. Trout's next three blows were absorbed by the captain's head, arm, and body, respectively. Trout worked on the body throughout the rest of the round, with an occasional blow to the head. The captain was only successful in blocking a small amount of the body punches. The bell sounded and the captain staggered back to his corner.

A Vendran in the captain's corner urged him to give up. Both left and right sides were bruised badly. The captain had bruises covering both arms, and a badly blackened right eye. He shook off the Vendran's suggestion and smiled. The second shrugged and replaced the mouthpiece for round two.

Round two began for Peter Trout the same as had round one. He moved across the ring quickly, eager to put his slow-moving captain out. Trout swung a wicked right cross that would have taken Traynor's head off if it had connected. But the captain was not where Trout expected. He had moved to his right much faster than Trout had expected. The result of the Vendran's effort was to throw himself several feet through the air. Trout regained his balance and located the captain in the ring. Moving forward, Trout repeated his performance, with the same results. Once again Traynor was not there. This time, when Trout regained his balance, he stopped to take stock. The captain was moving much quicker than before. Trout moved in slowly. He threw a left hook which was caught on the shoulder. A series of left jabs were picked off by gloves. A left-right comb to the body hit the captain's arms instead. Everything Trout threw was either blocked or sidestepped. Trout could not figure it out. An Earther should not be able to move that fast in Vendran gravity. And hadn't he been able to hit the captain when he pleased during the first round? Round two ended while he was still puzzling it out.

Round three, and the captain came out much quicker. Trout crossed the ring and threw a left, which was countered by a left-right combination to the head. Three lefts surprised Trout before he could lift his gloves. A right cross brought blood from Trout's nose.

Two rights to the body, a left to the head, and a straight right that caught him moving back, sent Trout to the floor. He was up in a flash, moved forward, and was sent to the canvas again by a furious exchange of lefts and rights to the head that left his head ringing. This time he stayed down, not because he couldn't get up, but because if he did get up, there was a good chance he would be down again. The captain had conned him, and he knew it.

"Before you believe hearsay, you should check all your facts," the Captain said. His second removed his gloves, and the captain crawled through the ropes and left the gymnasium.

Trout stood. His second came out to help, but he waved the man off. He quickly crossed over to a computer terminal.

"Computer, printout of service record, Traynor, Alexander, Captain USR *Polaris*." The others moved near the visiscreen. Slowly the computer began printing a list of Traynor's service posts. The most recent station caught Trout's eye. He called up more information on that particular station, the polar outpost on Epilson Sirius.

"Colonel Alexander Traynor, command Outpost Two, Epsilon Sirius," Trout read from the data sheet. "Epsilon Sirius: diameter twenty thousand forty kilometers. Gravity three point two four Earth." He skipped the next technical data. The men slowly began realizing a new respect for their captain. "Personnel of Outpost Two consisted of one Earther and four hundred seventy five Vendrans!" Slowly, very slowly, Peter Trout began to laugh. It took several moments for the others to understand the meaning of what Trout had read, but as the light began to dawn, they joined his laughter.

To live with almost five hundred Vendrans,

Traynor could not believe those statements attributed to him. Not and have survived his last tour of duty!

"That was extremely stupid, Alex!" De Gaulle scolded the captain. "You could have been beaten to a pulp!"

"I think I was," Traynor laughed. "Ow, that hurts."

"Serves you right!"

Traynor was in sickbay. He had staggered there before collapsing. De Gaulle had been summoned as Traynor was helped to a bed.

De Gaulle examined Traynor carefully as the captain explained painfully what had happened. He was a mass of body bruises, but fortunately his face had remained fairly normal, even under the terrific blows he had received. De Gaulle's examination showed five cracked ribs, along with a torn ligament in the captain's shoulder. Traynor complained of pain when he took a breath, which De Gaulle attributed to the cracked ribs.

"What do you mean, challenging a Vendran in heavy gravity?" De Gaulle demanded. "You'll get yourself killed doing that too often."

"It was something that was needed," Traynor replied seriously. "I had to get them to look at my files. I knew that if I told them to look, they'd make up some reason not to. And, if that rumor that started two days ago was taken seriously by the other outworlders, this ship could be in big trouble. I had to give the Vendrans a reason to check up on me. Don't you see Marc, it was the only way. I can't have men that I need distrustful of me!"

"I suppose so," De Gaulle agreed. He checked the instruments at the head of the bed. On one side was the electro-cardio monitor, monitoring heart activity. It read normal. Beside the ECM was the electro-encephalic monitor, showing brain activity. Also normal. Several other devices, for monitoring blood flow, lung expansion, and other bodily functions, recorded normal. The only abnormal reading on the instruments came from the skeletal continuity exam. A printout recorded the location and nature of the fractures to the captain's ribs.

The door to the examination room slid open as De Gaulle finished wrapping Traynor's chest with bandages. Two people entered. Traynor recognized them both instantly.

"How is he, Marc?" Hal Nater asked. The huge Ganymedan looked worried.

"He'll live," De Gaulle replied. "Nothing serious. Cracked ribs. I want him to stay here for a few hours and let the ribs start to knit under treatment. Not more than four or five hours."

"Good." Nater looked relieved.

"Hal, get hold of Goldman. He's the pilot on my shift. Tell him he has command of that shift until further notice. Let Angela Martin work as pilot."

"She's just a specialist," Nater reminded the captain. "Mr. Nelson might raise a stink."

"Tell him to see me," Traynor replied. "Marc, I'm not supposed to have any visitors during laser treatments, right?" He grinned. De Gaulle's face lit up in a broad smile.

"That's right," he said.

Traynor's second visitor moved closer.

"I'm glad you're all right, Captain," Erica LeMay said.

"I'm fine, Major," Traynor smiled at her. "And my name is Alex, Erica."

"Well, I've got more important things to do than sit here and listen to this," De Gaulle said indignantly. "I'll let someone else try to tell this fool captain not to take the whole universe on his shoulders." He stalked out.

"I've got to contact Goldman, sir," Nater said discreetly. "So of you'll excuse me." He exited quickly.

"Subtle, aren't they?" Traynor observed. Erica smiled. Slowly she began to giggle. Her giggles became laughter.

"Oh come now. It wasn't that funny," Traynor told her.

"It's not that," she replied. "You look like a half-dressed mummy." Which was true, for De Gaulle had wrapped the captain from armpit to waist with over a hundred meters of bandages and tape. He had also wrapped Traynor's right shoulder and strapped it to the captain's chest.

Outside the examining room, Nater pulled the doctor to one side.

"How is he? Really?"

"Just like I said. Cracked ribs." De Gaulle was not smiling now. "He's very lucky."

"How did it happen?" Nater asked. "An accident?"

"Not hardly. Boxing," De Gaulle answered. "Our glorious leader was making an effort to counteract the rumors that have been spreading concerning his opinion of Vendrans."

"You don't mean . . . " Nater began.

"You've got it. Him and a Vendran."

"You're kidding! At Earth grav, a Vendran would have torn him apart! One solid right would put an Earther in sickbay for a month." Nater said unbelievingly.

"He's not stupid, Hal," De Gaulle said. "He took on the Vendran in heavy grav. He does have some experience in that."

Nater paused for a moment, lost in thought. De Gaulle, too, was thinking. After several moments, De

Gaulle spoke.

"Something has to be done. If Alex has to take on someone from each outworld, literally, he'll never survive."

"That's true," Nater agreed. "Let me have the name of the man who did it to the Captain. I'll settle with him."

"I wouldn't worry about that man," De Gaulle laughed. "Being knocked down twice in one round by an Earther in Vendran gravity, in front of other Vendrans, is enough punishment."

Nater did not believe him.

"I have confirmation, Hal, but you can ask the fellow himself. Lieutenant Peter Trout."

"Peter? He's a close friend," Nater said, surprised. "I'll talk to him about it after I get in touch with Goldman and Martin."

Erica LeMay exited the examining room, blushing as she ran into the two men. She lowered her eyes to hide her embarrassment as she pushed past them and left sickbay.

"Well, he certainly won't have any difficulty with certain members of the crew," Nater said, his eyes twinkling.

"True," De Gaulle laughed.

The huge Ganymedan exited through the door Erica had used.

"What do you mean, boxing the Captain?" Hal Nater demanded.

"I didn't force him, Hal," Peter Trout replied.

The two security men sat sipping drinks in the crew's lounge. It was a huge room, filled with many off-duty personnel. Here could be heard the latest gossip from all the far parts of the ship. And the latest tidbit floating around the lounge was the news of the captain in sickbay.

"You must realize you could've killed him?" Nater said angrily.

"Look, Hal, don't jump on me," Trout replied defensively. "He didn't have to stand there and take it that first round. As easily as he put me down in the third, he could have done it in the first."

"Don't you see why he stood there and let you take your best shots?" Nater asked, still visibly upset. "He knew that your people were upset about the rumors circulating the ship. He stood there and let you, as a representative of all Vendrans, do your best to beat the hell out of him. And don't kid yourself. You busted him up pretty good."

"Yeah. Five cracked ribs and a torn ligament can be painful," Trout nodded. "I'll tell you this. I can still feel those shots to my head. I've never seen anyone move that fast in heavy grav that wasn't a Vendran."

"Well, the Captain will surprise you," Nater answered, calming down. "And it looks like he did give you a good shot or two. You'd better take care of that eye." Trout touched the area just below his right eye. It was puffy and dark, swollen to twice its normal size.

"It'll be OK in a day or so," the Vendran replied.

A young Collierite, blue-eyed and freckle faced, came over to the table. He wore lieutenant's stripes and a patch identifying him as a medical technician.

"Excuse me, Lieutenant Trout, but is it true that you had it out with the Captain in the gym, and beat him silly?"

"I was afraid of this," Nater told his friend.

"We'll solve this problem quickly," Trout laughed. He picked up his drink from the table and handed it to Nater. Then he climbed onto the tabletop. He stamped his foot loudly and began to yell. Slowly the room became silent, as everyone within turned to regard the fellow standing on his table.

"Thank you so much for giving me your attention," Trout shouted. "I'm sorry to interrupt you, but I feel I should set the latest rumor straight before it goes too far. While it is true that I boxed Captain Traynor, it is not true that I beat him. After receiving my strongest punches, and suffering five cracked ribs, Captain Traynor was able to knock me down twice, in such a way as to preclude my continuing. If I'd gotten back up, he'd have knocked me down again.

"Now, I can see from your faces that you don't believe me. Well, unless you would like to tell fifteen Vendran security men that they are liars, believe. And, if any of you are thinking of doing the same thing, forget it. You have to fight me first." Hal Nater stood, implying that he would also block any of the crew from duplicating Trout's actions.

The crew in the room looked at the two men standing at the center of attention, and their expressions became respectful. They returned to their activities, much to the delight of the two security men.

"That's telling 'em, Peter," Nater congratulated the Vendran. Trout turned and looked at his friend, tilting his head slightly downward, and flashing a broad smile.

"You know, this is the first time I've ever looked down at you, Hal." Trout jumped down from the table and they both sat down, laughing.

IV

Robert Goldman sat in the command chair, occupied with the visual representation of the planet Kappa Barnard, projected on the big screen. Small representations of the huge sub-fleet that orbited the planet were also present on the screen.

Goldman was working his third watch as duty commander, and he had performed admirably. His watches had been routine in that there had been no activity in the area of space around 'the Rock.'

This watch was of particular significance to Goldman, for Captain Traynor had arrived shortly after the shift had begun. Goldman had stepped away from the command chair, but the captain waved him back. Traynor explained that he was not present to relieve the young man, just to observe. The captain seated himself at the vacant executive officer's console.

One of the requirements of the duty commander was to visually locate and record into the computer the whereabouts of the patrolling sub-fleet on the map representation. Regulations required it done within the first hour of watch. Goldman, Traynor noted with approval, had waited thirty minutes, allowing the new personnel to adjust to being on duty. Now he was fulfilling the regulation. Traynor smiled. "Just the way I do it," he thought.

Young Robert Goldman rechecked the coordinates

twice, as if his life depended on it. And it was his life; the Republic's Space Service. Goldman, twenty-nine, had been with the service for ten years, since joining on his nineteenth birthday. He had left his home world, Iapetus, one of the larger moons of Saturn.

Iapetus was settled in 2095 by a group of scientists and doctors dedicated to psychic research. Psychic research had been conducted for nearly four hundred years. In those years, the psychic ability of the people of Iapetus had grown to rival the abilities of the people of Pronetha.

Once a child reached his eighteenth birthday, he was sent to the Psychic Research Academy. Every student was tested and classified in terms of natural ability, latent ability, and inclination. Robert Goldman had received the lowest classification ranking ever given by the PRA of Iapetus. Because of the disgrace to his family, Goldman had run from the PRA and joined the Space Service.

The only other Iapetan member of *Polaris*'s crew was the navigator of Goldman's watch, Commander Maria McMasters. Medium height, blonde, two years older than Goldman, she had tested at the PRA and received one of the highest classification ratings ever. She graduated first in her class at the PRA, and then joined the Space Service on a whim. At the Service Academy she met Robert Goldman, who was a classmate. Since it was rare for an Iapetan to join the Space Service, and even rarer for two, a natural closeness developed between the two. They had strived, successfully, to serve together during their seven years of active duty since the academy.

Traynor had marvelled at the way they often functioned—as if possessing one brain. When he had rechecked the proper files concerning the two, Traynor reasoned that they often shared the same thoughts.

Goldman finished the sub-fleet location drill and was beginning to check the different sections when he was interrupted by Lieutenant Mary Stuart, the communications specialist on duty.

"Captain, I'm picking something up. Just barely audible."

Traynor glanced to Goldman, watching to see if the young commander would allow the obvious disregard of regulations to slip by. Goldman spun the command chair to face the girl.

"Put it on audio, *Lieutenant*," he said icily. The young Lunarite quickly obeyed orders. Maria Mc Masters glanced toward the captain, who smiled and winked at her. She returned his smile, then focused her attention on the instruments before her.

"It's on, sir," Lieutenant Stuart told Goldman.

"Mayday! Emergency!" came from the speakers on the bridge. "USR *Moscow* calling any USR ship! Emergency! We have been under attack! Ship disabled! Emergency! Ship disabled! Emergency! USR *Moscow* calling any USR ship! Need assistance! Ship disabled!" The hysterical voice on the speakers died out. Goldman went over to the communications console. Stuart shook her head.

"Nothing, sir."

Traynor watched his young officer carefully, noting how he handled the emergency, and ready to jump in at any moment if Goldman should slip.

"Colonel N'goto, did you get a fix on that message?" Goldman asked.

"I'm working on it now," the black replied. "It should take only a moment, Commander."

"Good, sir." Goldman again turned to Lieutenant Stuart. "Raise Admiral Willoby aboard *Pearl Harbor*." Stuart busily set about contacting the flagship of the sub-fleet.

N'goto and Stuart reached their goals at precisely the same moment.

"Admiral Willoby on the big screen, sir," Stuart said. N'goto quickly crossed over and whispered to Goldman his success in coming up with approximate coordinates for the distress call. N'goto also whispered to the captain, still seated at the exec console, as the big screen lit up. Admiral Willoby's face filled the screen.

The admiral was a large man with a broad face and thick neck. His blond hair, graying slightly at the temples, was cut short and neatly combed. The most remarkable feature of the Admiral's face were his piercing blue eyes.

"Commander Robert Goldman, duty commander of *Polaris*, sir," Goldman identified himself.

"Yes, Commander?" the admiral asked quickly.

"Sir, our communications officer just picked up a distress call from a USR ship identifying itself as *Moscow*."

"Where's your captain? Is he aware you are contacting me? Is he aware of the distress call?" the admiral growled.

"Yes sir, I am," Traynor quickly answered. "I was here when the message was received and the order to contact you given. Mr. Goldman performed precisely as regulations demand."

"Very good. Commander, you are the second ship to report receiving a distress message from *Moscow*," Admiral Willoby informed Goldman. "The scout ship *Marrakesh* received a partial signal, but not enough to get a fix."

"Sir, Colonel N'goto, science officer on duty, has computed an approximate location," Goldman replied triumphantly.

"Very good, Commander," Willoby nodded approvingly. "I can only spare one ship to investigate.

Since you have the coordinates, you get the job." His voice became solemn. "You're on your own. If there are still any enemy craft around, it's up to you to do as you see fit." Goldman nodded.

"Good luck. Willoby out."

"*Polaris* out," Goldman answered. "Captain, maybe you'd better take over."

"Carry out the Admiral's orders," Traynor replied.

"Yes, sir!" Goldman said excitedly. He turned to face the main screen.

"Miss McMasters, have you received the coordinates?"

"Coordinates received and course computed," she answered crisply.

"Miss Martin, lock in and implement; full battle speed."

"Aye, sir," Angela Martin replied. The ship accelerated out of orbit, executing a smooth one-hundred-and-eighty-degree turn under the careful guidance of the young pilot.

"Computer identification of USR *Moscow*, Commander," N'goto said softly. He had returned to his station to the right and forward of the command chair.

"Good. Let's have a look at what we're hunting for," Goldman replied. "Put it on the screen please, sir." The science officer complied.

"*Moscow* is a destroyer of the *Lincoln* class," N'goto recited. "Overall length three hundred ten meters. One hull, one neutronium-drive generator. Crew of two forty-three. Present commander Colonel Fahlen Kilter of Oberon."

"Thank you, Colonel," Goldman said, after studying the vessel for a moment. "Maria, how soon to the projected coordinates?"

"One hour, forty-two minutes," the Iapetan girl

replied.

"Good. Sound Yellow Alert, Lieutenant Stuart," Goldman ordered.

"Aye, sir." The buzzer, signifying Yellow Alert, sounded, accompanied by a flashing yellow light above the main visiscreen. Yellow lights on each deck, in each corridor, throughout the ship, would be flashing in a similar manner. Every inch of the ship was penetrated by the alert buzzer.

For seventy-five minutes *Polaris* stayed on Yellow Alert. At minus twenty-seven minutes, *Polaris* went on Red Alert. The ship's sensors probed to their furthest reaches, searching for any indication of the vessel in distress.

Captain Traynor decided the call to Red Alert was the time to take command. He relieved Goldman, who replaced Angela Martin at the pilot console. She in turn, headed for the hangar deck. Carl Nelson assumed his position at the exec console.

At minus two minutes N'goto informed the captain of sensor contact of two vessels at extreme range: two degrees to port and three degrees below the ship's horizon. McMasters and Goldman, working smoothly as a team, corrected *Polaris*'s course without verbal command from the captain.

"Captain, I have them on scanner," Stuart informed Traynor, after three minutes on the corrected course.

"Put them on the screen,' Traynor commanded. The main screen's image changed from a picture of the immediate space before the ship to an image of space four billion kilometers ahead.

"Prepare to come out of neutronium drive in one minute," Traynor told the bridge. He studied the action on the screen as the image became larger. Stuart changed magnification as the image became too large.

Two ships hung motionless in space. One was *Moscow*, easily identifiable from the representation the bridge personnel had viewed earlier. The second craft had lines similar to *Moscow*, but the bridge crew quickly recognized that the second ship had not been built at a USR space yard.

"Cut to sublight," Traynor ordered. "Shields up! Sensors three-sixty by three-sixty constant! I don't want anyone sneaking up on us! Secondary sensors probe those ships!" Traynor's voice was clear and cool, calming the nervous youngsters that made up the bulk of the bridge crew.

"*Moscow* reads one hundred seventeen life forms at various points on the ship," N'goto informed the captain. "Forty-eight on the hangar deck. Seventeen in a lab on 'B' deck. Fourteen in engineering. Six in the weapons section, and the remainder in the sickbay. Power in life support systems only."

"Enemy vessel?" Traynor glanced over to the science officer.

"No power that I can read. No life forms of our type. Sensors do not seem to be able to probe the ship with any accuracy. Something is disrupting the probes."

"We'll worry about that later. First priority is to get the people off *Moscow*."

"Sir, we're as close as possible without dropping our shields," Goldman spoke up.

"All stop. Hold us here, Goldman," Traynor ordered. "Shipwide, Lieutenant Stuart."

She quickly thumbed the switch open.

"Shipwide, sir."

"This is the captain," Traynor began. "*Moscow* is sitting out there, just outside our shields. It's a dead ship, powerwise. Sensors pick up one hundred seventeen life forms out of a crew of two hundred forty-three.

"Also just outside our shields is an enemy vessel—a

destroyer, if its size is any clue. It seems to be in the same condition as *Moscow*. Seems to be. Our sensors are not able to successfully penetrate the ship with any accuracy. All they tell us is there is no power available on the ship.

"I am preparing to send out rescue crews to *Moscow*. Captain out.

"Stuart, security, then the hangar deck."

"Security here," came a voice from Traynor's chair-arm console.

"Mark, I need three rescue teams on the hangar deck in three minutes. Deep-space work suits, a bubble for each crew, and cutting tools," Traynor ordered. "Eight-man crews ought to do it."

"Aye, sir," Carter answered. He signed off.

"Hangar deck," came the response to Traynor's call.

"Myra, we need three large birds readied. Rescue crews are assembling down there in two and a half minutes. Also, clear out an area where the medical section can work on the seriously injured brought in."

"Is that a good idea?" she asked.

"It might save a life," Traynor responded.

"Aye, sir," Shanesey agreed, somewhat reluctantly. "Out."

"Out." Traynor stood up and hurried to the elevator. "N'goto, on me. Nelson, you have the con. I'll be on the hangar deck. Stuart, call De Gaulle and get him down there on the double. Then get hold of Marshall and get him up here!" The two men entered the elevator without waiting for responses.

On the hangar deck twenty-four security men were zipping into their deep-space work suits, used for operations carried out in the airless void of space. A fourth crew of security men helped the rescue parties suit up.

The work suits were of form-fitting clear plastic that allowed a minutely thin layer of oxygen to remain constantly between the suit and the wearer. The helmet was molded from the same plastic, though it was not pliable, as was the suit. The helmet fastened to a collar of similar construction; the only nonpliable part of the body suit. A recycling air-supply container was constructed into the helmet, directly behind the head. Once activated, the small container provided seven days' use without loss of recycling capability.

Myra Shanesey and her entire crew of technicians checked and rechecked the three rescue ships, scrambling over their bodies, digging into the engines, and checking over controls and power generators, until the captain made his appearance on the deck.

Traynor hurried over to the supervisor, who was crawling out of the engine hatch of *Discovery*, the largest of the fifteen craft available. Lieutenants Jay Farnsworth III and David Emerson came up to the captain and the commander.

"*Providence* checks out," Farnsworth informed the two.

"*Friendship* the same," Emerson echoed.

"Good," Myra answered. "Now, do it again!"

"Aye, ma'am," they replied, hustling back to their charges.

"Are they ready, Commander?" Traynor asked.

"As they'll ever be," she replied confidently.

"Good." Traynor nodded approval. "Squad commanders!" Five men hurried foreward. Three wore pressure suits. Traynor recognized three of the men as Mark Carter, Peter Trout, and Hal Nater. The two new faces were identified as those of Travis Dralen of Vendra and Mikhail Noverensky of Collier. Trout, Nater, and Noverensky wore the work suits.

"You've been briefed on the layout of *Moscow*?"

Traynor asked. The men nodded. Traynor and N'goto quickly briefed the men on the plan of attempted rescue.

Nater, commanding the squad aboard *Discovery*, would erect a pressure dome on the side of *Moscow*, outside the hangar deck. They were to cut an entrance into the hangar deck and check the feasibility of opening a hangar lock to allow *Discovery* to dock. If not, Nater's squad was to erect a pressure tube and transport the survivors from *Moscow's* hangar deck to *Discovery*, and back to *Polaris*.

Trout, aboard *Providence*, was to erect a dome near the tail of the crippled ship, on the upper side of the hull. Once inside, their objective was *Moscow*'s sickbay. A pressure tube to *Providence* would be the escape route.

The third team, Noverensky aboard *Friendship*, would duplicate *Providence*'s actions, but at the forward end of the hull. Their objective was the weapons section and a certain lab on "B" deck, which were three rooms apart. Noverensky's team would also use a pressure tube between ships.

Once the main objective was achieved, each team was to turn its attention to reaching the engineering section of *Moscow*, which was located on "C" deck of the five-decked hull.

"And the ships will have returned by the time you reach the engineering section," Traynor concluded. "Now remember, first crew there calls off the others. Immediately!

"Work fast. We don't know how long before our little friend out there may be joined by his friends. Good luck." They saluted him and the three mission commanders hustled to their respective crews. Quickly, the ships were loaded and the launch procedure was underway.

Marc De Gaulle came hurrying through the entrance. He rushed up to Traynor.

"What do you need?"

"Get your crew set up down here," Traynor replied. "You may have over a hundred casualties and this is the only place big enough. Don't know. Haven't been able to raise *Moscow*."

"But there may be critical cases," De Gaulle began.

"All the more reason to be here. They may not live to get to sickbay," Traynor answered quickly. "Get your people moving, Marc."

"Now that you mention it, this would be a nice place to work," De Gaulle smiled weakly.

Traynor smiled apologeticly.

"I knew you'd see it my way, Marc." He crossed over to where Myra Shanesey was supervising the launch of the rescue ships. She quickly informed the captain that *Discovery* and *Providence* were away, and *Friendship* was preparing to cut in its forward drive.

"Excellent work, Commander Shanesey," Traynor grinned. "Remind me, when this is over, I owe you a drink. You've got one hell of a launch crew!" She matched his grin.

"Ye kin bank on it, Captain," she answered, slipping into her Ioan brogue.

"I'll be on the bridge," he told her.

On the bridge, a problem had arisen. After the arrival of Theodore Marshall to assume the bridge duties of the science officer, Victoria Spencer and Ben Peters had arrived. They immediately went to their command stations, expecting to take over. The two Iapetans, however, refused to relinquish their seats. Maria McMasters informed her superior that she would only give up the navigation controls on direct orders from the captain. Goldman added that he agreed fully.

Carl Nelson, acting bridge commander, stepped

down from the chair at Goldman's words.

"You realize that you are disobeying an order from your direct superior?" he asked. They both replied affirmatively.

"Then," he continued, "I am giving you a direct order, as a Colonel in the Space Service, to vacate your posts and allow your bet—, uh, superiors, to take over."

Both Maria McMasters and Robert Goldman were shocked at the slip of the tongue by Nelson. They exchanged glances, as if probing each other's thoughts—which, being Iapetans, they were actually doing. Goldman then turned his chair to face the angry executive officer.

"Colonel Nelson," he said slowly. "To comply with your orders, I would have to disobey orders issued to me by a captain of the Space Service, which I will not do."

Nelson fairly exploded at the calm assurance of the young man.

"I have given you a direct order, Mister!" he screamed. "If you don't obey it, I'll have you up before a review board on a mutiny charge before you can count three!"

"Any mutiny charges will have to go through me," a calm voice sounded behind Nelson. He turned angrily and stopped. Alexander Traynor sat in the command chair, arriving unnoticed to the Executive Officer.

"Sir, according to regulations, the senior officer of each section is to man the controls!" Nelson screamed. "These two outworlders won't move, disobeying direct orders from myself and Majors Spencer and Peters!"

"Colonel, I told them they would finish this job."

"Sir, you can't let them get away with this!" Nelson continued, still screaming. "Ben and Victoria must take over! You know that! Issue the orders!"

Slowly Traynor rose from his chair to face the enraged executive officer. They stood toe to toe, eye to eye.

"Nelson," the Captain began, straining to remain under control. "No one tells me how to run my ship. NO ONE!" I do what I think is best for the good of the ship, not any one person. Don't ever make that mistake again. Do I make myself clear?"

The fire was still in Nelson, but he realized that he was in no position to argue. He nodded his head.

"Good," Traynor responded. "You are relieved of duty and confined to quarters until tomorrow at 0900 hours when you will report to my quarters. We have a few things to discuss." Nelson came to attention, saluted, and exited. Traynor settled back into his seat.

"*Discovery* calling," Lieutenant Stuart spoke up, breaking the silence.

"Put 'em on," Traynor answered. "You're monitoring all frequencies?"

"Aye, sir."

"Captain, we are alongside *Moscow*," Angela Martin's clear voice sang out. "Lieutenant Nater and his men are leaving now." Traynor gazed at the big screen. *Moscow* dominated the picture. From the angle of the picture,, *Discovery* could not be seen. *Providence* and *Friendship* were in evidence, moving carefully into their assigned positions.

"Hal, can you hear me?" Traynor spoke into is chair-arm console.

"Loud and clear, sir," came the voice of the giant Ganymedan.

"We can't see you, so keep us informed as to what you are doing," the Captain ordered.

"Aye, sir," Nater replied.

Slowly the crew from *Discovery* jetted to the hull of *Moscow*. Once they reached the metallic hull, their boot magnets took hold, allowing the men to stand. In relation to the ship, the eight men were standing parallel to the decks. But there is no up or down in space. Therefore, wherever one's feet are is down, and where one's head is should then be up.

Once each member of the crew was firmly anchored to the hull, Nater ordered the equipment lines dragged in. The weightless containers were dragged into the waiting arms of the rescue crew.

Peter Trout's crew, aboard *Providence*, was in the process of debarking. The pilot had landed the ship on the hull of *Moscow*. In actuality, the rescue ship was hovering ten centimeters above the hull. Trout's squad bounded quickly out of *Providence*. Instantly their boots gripped the injured craft in a magnetic lock. With the crew and equipment unloaded, *Providence* moved away a safe distance to await a call from Trout to engage the pressure tube.

"Trout to *Polaris*," the young Vendran radioed. His squad began to unload and erect the pressure dome from the magnetically secured equipment containers.

"*Polaris*, Traynor here," sounded the radio.

"Preparing to erect pressure dome, sir," Trout reported.

"Peter, Mikhail," came over the radio. It was Hal Nater calling.

"Yeah, Hal," Trout answered. Noverensky's voice sounded also.

"Check your hull wiring programs carefully before cutting. We just cut through a wire that really gave us a shock."

"Anyone hurt?" Traynor interrupted.

"No, Captain, just a nice display of fireworks for a few seconds."

"Good." Traynor was relieved. "Watch yourselves."

"Careful, Hal," Trout told Nater. Noverensky also added something, though Trout could not hear.

"Thanks, Mik," came Nater's sarcastic response.

Friendship duplicated *Providence's* actions in landing on the forward end of the hull. Here they ran into a problem. All crew members quickly exited the craft, but when the equipment containers were unloaded, one of the cylinders did not magnetically fasten to the hull. A squad member, ignorant of the cylinder not being attached, bumped the equipment as he moved past. In the weightlessness of space, that slight bump was enough to send the container out into open space, some hundred meters from *Moscow*.

"Trouble, skipper," one of the men informed Noverensky.

"What's the problem, Lieutenant Noverensky?" Traynor's voice sounded quickly.

"One of the cylinders' magnetic coupler apparently didn't energize," answered the squad leader. "Johnson, can you get it?"

The young man guilty of causing the cylinder's floating antics quickly responded affirmatively.

"Careful, Johnson," Traynor commanded. "Make sure you have a line."

"Aye, sir," replied Johnson. Two others attached the line from the second cylinder to Johnson's back hook. The other end of the line was hooked to the fastened cylinder, but two companions gripped the line as added insurance.

Johnson jetted out to the free-floating cylinder, hanging in space. Gripping the container tightly, he attempted to jet back, all the while wondering what had caused the cylinder to stop its free flight. Theoretically, the container should have continued on its way until it was deflected by something. His jets should have been powerful enough to push the container back to

Moscow. However, even firing at three-quarters power, he could not move the cylinder.

"Mik, I can't move it," Johnson radioed.

"What do you mean, can't move it?" Noverensky replied.

"Something's holding it!"

"That's me," the pilot of *Friendship* came on the radio to say, "I grabbed it with the mini-tractor. It's a good thing I'm in one of the bigger ships. The smaller ones don't have mini-tracs. That thing would be long gone by now."

Friendship released its grip on the container and Johnson navigated the cylinder back to his crew. Willing hands grabbed the cylinder and fastened it tightly to its companion, using the line that had been recently attached to Lieutenant Johnson.

"Ready to erect pressure dome, Captain," Noverensky reported.

"Go to it."

The pressure dome was a very important piece of equipment in the field of exterior ship repair. Made of clear plastic similar to the material the work suits were constructed from, though much thicker, the clear dome was erected around the work area. Measuring from five to twenty meters in diameter, depending on use, the dome allowed work to be performed on the exterior of a ship within an atmospheric seal. Because of the seal, the compartments within did not have to be evacuated.

"Captain, we're through," Hal Nater notified Traynor.

"How's it look?" Traynor asked.

"Checking." was Nater's response. Still wearing his work suit, for safety as well as to remain in constant radio contact, Nater carefully inserted his head and shoulders through the opening the cutters had made. Quickly, Nater's head pulled back.

"My God!" he whispered.

"What's wrong, Hal?" Traynor asked over the radio.

"The hangar deck. You've got to see it to believe it! I never knew there could be so much destruction aboard one ship! Even *Polaris* wasn't this bad!"

"There are supposed to be forty-eight people in there," Nater was reminded. "You see any?"

"I'll tell you in a moment," Nater radioed. "We're going in." He slipped through the opening and dropped to the deck, eight feet down. The gravity of *Moscow* was still in effect, which allowed Nater and the others to de-energize their magnetic boot soles. The lights in the hanger were not fully operational.

Nater switched to loudspeaker broadcast. "Hello. Anyone here?" A dozen or so figures moved out of the machinery strung around the room, to stand in the semi-glow of the hanger lights. "We're from the USR *Polaris*."

Several men and women came rushing up to hug Nater.

"Thank God someone finally came!" one woman cried.

"Captain," Nater radioed. "We've got some survivors."

"Very good, Hal," Traynor replied. In the background Nater could hear controlled cheering from the bridge crew of *Polaris*.

"Olson, start on the aft door. Hadrada and Vahlar, start on the main doors. We need to start for the engineering section. Devars, check the docking mechanisms. I don't think they'll work, but we might as well try. The rest of you start looking for survivors. There are forty-eight here." Nater paused. "I count thirteen now. Get these people to help you."

Peter Trout radioed *Polaris*.

"We're through, Captain. Preparing to drop into the corridor." He eased through the opening his crew's energy cutters had made, and dropped to the cluttered floor.

"I'm down. Corridor twelve, deck A. It's really messy down here. Debris all around my feet. Can't see anything. No lights. Tovar, lower me a light."

"Right, Peter," Tovar Mehatma replied. The light was lowered to Trout's waiting hands. Trout fastened it to the mount on the top of his helmet. Turning his head from side to side, he was able to play the beam around the corridor.

"It's messy, fellas. Don't be surprised to see bodies," Trout informed his crew. "Come on down. Bring the cutters. And a light for everyone."

The squad came down, one at a time. Each moved out and forward, playing his light over the area forward of their position.

"OK, let's move," Trout ordered, when the others had dropped to the deck. Trout led the way, searching for the ladder to "B" deck.

"Trout, what's it look like?" Traynor asked.

"It's pretty torn up in here," Trout replied, picking his way through the debris. "Walls caved in. Machinery across the corridor, but we aren't blocked. No tears in the outer skin. Apparently the auto-sealing equipment is still functioning. Bodies. Quite a few. Several quite disfigured. Must have been hit by enemy lasers. That explains the other bodies. The oxygen must have escaped when the laser cut through. Killed the others before the sealing equipment could save 'em."

"Skipper, this one is still alive!" the last man in line exclaimed.

"Can't be, Fedar," Trout replied. He stopped and waved the others to pass. Then he moved back to where

Fedar Mohand, his Vendran muscles easily handling the massive weight of the energy cutters strapped to his back, knelt beside one of *Moscow's* crew.

"Peter, I swear I saw her move!" Mohand continued vehemently.

"OK. We can't take any chances," Trout decided. "Captain, we've got a possible survivor that wasn't expected. We'll be sending her immediately. You'd better send another ship. We'll be sending *Providence* back now."

"Check. *Dawnstar* will be there in moments. You need any more help?"

"Not at the moment, sir," Trout replied. "But have them standing by in case." Trout turned and motioned to one of the waiting men. "O'Hanrahan, you take her to the bubble. Jorgenson will hook in the pressure tube and you can take this young lady to the ship."

O'Hanrahan lifted the woman and started back the way they had come.

"The Z-grav belts will give you enough neutralization to lift both of you through the opening. And tell Jorgenson that she's to get you back as quick as possible. Hear that, Carol Ann?"

"Peter, have I ever let you down?" a soft voice purred through the squad commander's speakers. "Get your man up here."

O'Hanrahan moved out of view as one of the men forward gave a shout.

"Got it, skipper!" René Millerand cried. He motioned Trout to an opening on the left side of the corridor. "It looks clear."

"This is the one," Trout agreed. "Down." He began climbing down the ladder.

The third rescue team was having more problems. After securing their equipment cylinder, they had run into difficulty setting up the dome. Once that problem was solved, they began cutting, only to cut through a wire not listed on Noverensky's wiring reference program. The energy flash knocked Lieutenant Michael Todd senseless for several minutes. He recovered without any other effects than a bruise on the back of his head when he flipped backwards.

Because of delays and accidents, Noverensky was dropping into the corridor below while the other teams were involved with the actual rescue of *Moscow* personnel. Noverensky surveyed the corridor he had dropped into, flashing his light back and forth across the expanse.

"Problems again," he sighed disgustedly. "Both directions blocked."

"Not passable at all?" Traynor's voice questioned.

"It would take several hours to clear either direction," replied Noverensky.

"Mik, this is Trout," came a voice in Noverensky's ear.

"What, Peter?"

"We're on 'B' deck. It's fairly clear, what we've been through. Of course, we're aft quite a ways from where you are, but we didn't have any great difficulty. Just loose junk and some bodies in the corridors immediately around the sick bay."

"Roger. We'll cut through to 'B' deck. Captain we'll need the wiring programs for this section, between 'A' and 'B' decks," Noverensky requested.

"Just a second," Traynor responded. To someone on the bridge: "Ready to send?" Apparently he received an affirmative, for he next spoke to Noverensky. "Ready to receive, Lieutenant?"

Noverensky removed the miniature self-contained computer terminal hanging at his waist.

"Ready, sir," he replied. The terminal in his hand

lit up. Quickly he scanned the tiny viewscreen, then motioned where his crew was to cut.

On the hangar deck of *Polaris*, things were beginning to happen. *Providence* was barely away after delivering the injured girl from *Moscow*, when *Discovery* arrived with a load of injured survivors.

Six operating tables had been sent up to one of the huge rooms. Medical technicians had set up and were monitoring the most sophisticated medical equipment available. The doctors awaited the casualties aboard *Discovery*—all the doctors save De Gaulle, who was busy with the first arrival.

As the injured were carefully lifted from the rescue ship, Marge Upshaw, the head nurse, categorized each into urgent, serious, and non-serious. The urgent cases were taken to the waiting doctors. The serious were looked after by the nurses not involved in assisting the doctors. Medical technicians aided the non-serious, applying antiseptic and bandages. Once she had ascertained that the wounded from *Discovery*'s first run had been taken care of, Major Upshaw wandered over to Marc De Gaulle's table. Major Hildy Bennett was assisting him on the young woman *Providence* had brought in.

"How's it coming, Marc?"

"I think she's going to make it, by God!" De Gaulle exclaimed. "I'm finished for now. Stretcher!" Two young lieutenants, a man and a girl, rushed up with a Z-grav stretcher. Carefully, the two, with De Gaulle and Bennett helping, lifted the young woman onto the platform. De Gaulle gave instructions for her care and sent them on their way to sick bay.

"What's next?" De Gaulle asked.

"A boy that caught a falling landing craft with his chest," Marge replied disgustedly.

"Let's do it." Marge nodded and stretcher bearers placed the injured boy on the table.

"Have someone check the proximity sterilizer," De Gaulle ordered, turning to the boy on the table.

"Marge!" A nurse screamed. "I've got a full arrest!"

"Marge!" A second voice sounded. "This girl is bleeding internally!"

"Get her on a table!" Marge called back. "Bridget, hook in the electro-cardio stimulator! On max!" She rushed to where Mercy Thompson and Liz Beaumont were lifting a young girl on to a free table.

"What happened?" Marge asked.

"She was fine, ma'am," Thompson explained. "You told me to patch up her small cuts and scrapes. I was doing that when she began choking."

"She called me Marge," Commander Beaumont took up the story. "I started to examine her when she began spitting up blood. That's when I called you."

The head nurse had been carefully watching the instruments hooked into the girl as she listened to the story.

"OK," she said. "Doctor!" All answered that they were busy. Staring at the instruments, Marge realized that the girl might not live until a doctor could get at her.

"We'll do it ourselves," she decided. Quickly she began issuing orders. "Get an intra-trachea tube in her! Keep her breathing! Keep her lungs clear!"

"Aye, ma'am," the young technician responded, racing for the instruments, which were across the room.

"Have you ever performed X-ray surgery?" Liz Beaumont asked.

"No," Marge replied, lifting a surgical kit to a Z-grav platform top beside the operating table. "That's why I'm going to have to open her up."

"I haven't assisted in open surgery since my first year in school, over eight years ago," Liz informed her superior.

"Don't worry," the Collierite replied. "It's just like riding a jet cycle. Once you learn, you never forget."

Thompson returned with the proper instruments, and proceeded to insert the airway. Suction kept the lungs clear.

"All set, Major," the youngster said, shakily.

Slowly, using an electro-knife, Marge cut into the chest of the injured girl. The electro-knife, its blade a beam of energy, cauterized the incision as it was made. Once through the skin, she checked the ribs. Four fractures on the left side, two on the right. A fifth rib on the left side had broken and become lodged in the lung.

"How's she doing?"

"OK as can be expected," Beaumont replied. "Can you stop the bleeding?"

"I think so. Forceps." Liz handed her the tool.

Marge tuned the knife for a fine cut. Gingerly, she gripped the rib with the forceps, close to where it entered the lung. Carfully, Marge cut through the rib at a point just above the forceps. The rib came apart cleanly. Marge set the electro-knife down.

"Internal electro-seal," she said. The instrument was instantly in her hand. She clicked it on and held it close to the lung, through an opening in the rib cage. Her finger sat softly on the activator, not releasing the healing power of the tool. Slowly she drew the piece of rib from the lung, activating the electro-seal immediately upon withdrawal of the bone fragment.

Major Francis Jenkins came hurrying up.

"What's going on?" he demanded.

"Close her up, Jenkins, and don't open your mouth!" Marge growled, stepping away from the girl.

"She'll live for now. It's not critical anymore." Slowly, Major Marge Upshaw stepped over to the doctor's tables. Liz Beaumont followed her when Jenkins had finished with the injured girl.

"That was fantastic, Marge!" Liz cried. Marge breathed a deep sigh.

"What was fantastic?" Marc De Gaulle asked, coming over from his table. He was taking a break while his nurse and technician prepped the next case.

"Marge just opened up a girl who was bleeding inside. She was great!" Liz explained. "The girl's going to be OK. I hadn't assisted on an open surgery for over eight years, but she said it was just like riding a jet cycle. She was right. I haven't forgotten. Just haven't done it in a while."

"Excellent, m'lady!" De Gaulle exclaimed. He stepped up and planted a kiss on Marge's lips before she could react, then hurried back to his table. Marge Upshaw, caught off guard, blushed a brilliant red. Liz Beaumont discreetly turned her head until her superior had recovered.

"Marge!" a voice rang out.

"Well, back to the grind," the woman sighed. "Confidentially, Liz, I never could ride a jet cycle." She grinned and hurried to answer the summons.

"We're finally through to 'B' deck," Noverensky radioed the captain. "Preparing to drop down."

"Go careful, Lieutenant," Traynor cautioned over the radio.

"Peterson, then Carson, after me in that order. The others wait until we check it out down there," Noverensky ordered. He rechecked the area immediately under the opening and, cautioning the others to keep a light on the deck below, dropped easily down. Fred Peterson and Jack Carson, two Lunarites in the crew, dropped in quick succession.

"What's it look like Mik?" Kevin Johnson asked.

"Not too bad," came the reply. "I'm moving down the corridor, and it seems pretty clear. Carson and Peterson are with me. Carson, check the other direction. So far it's clear. Prepare to drop . . . AIEEEE!"

Alex Traynor sat up quickly. He had been monitoring Noverensky's frequency and had heard the scream. An anxious look came over his face.

"Lieutenant Noverensky," he said. "Noverensky, come in. Come in!" He paused, but received no reply. "Noverensky, come in! Mikhail!" Still no response.

"Johnson here, sir," came a voice.

"What happened to Noverensky?" Traynor demanded.

"Don't know, sir," Johnson replied. "Can't see him, Peterson or Carson. They were together on 'B' deck. Can't raise any of them."

"Listen carefully, Johnson," Traynor said, still edgy. "One man, I repeat, one man, drop down to 'B' deck. Do not move from directly under the hole. Look around and see if you can find out what happened."

The bridge crew had stopped what they were doing and were listening intently. Traynor motioned to Lieutenant Stuart.

"Contact the hangar deck. Tell Dralen to get his crew aboard an LC and get over to *Moscow*. I'll give him his orders depending on what happens with the *Friendship* crew."

"Captain," Johnson called to *Polaris*. "I'm down. Beginning to sweep the corridor with my light and, there's one of them! A wall fell on him!"

"OK, Johnson, good. Don't panic." Traynor had noticed the slight change in Johnson's voice, possibly preluding a loss of control. "Don't go to them yet! Check the walls and ceiling. Is there a chance they'll fall on you?"

"Aye, sir, I'm checking." Johnson was calming down. "Right wall, ceiling and floor seams still intact to the gap where it fell on him. Section is about five meters long. Left wall, ceiling and floor seams intact for about ten meters past fallen section."

"Anything else?" Traynor asked.

"Not evident, sir," replied Johnson.

"*Darkstar* away, Captain," reported Stuart.

"Thank you, Lieutenant," acknowledged Traynor. "Johnson, bring your crew down. Carefully! Watch yourselves. Moving slowly and carefully, make your way down to the injured man. Try to lift the wall off them. Use caution! You may have to use a Z-grav lifter if the wall's too heavy."

"Aye, sir," Johnson replied. "They're coming down now." Traynor listened intently as the members of the depleted *Friendship* squad called off as they dropped deeper into *Moscow*. Todd, Davis, McDaniels, and Trovonski. Each was screened for traces of panic. Only Johnson showed any traces of panic, but that was natural, having had command of the squad thrust upon him so suddenly.

"We're moving down the corridor. It's not far. About three meters more. Todd is there already. Which one?"

"It's Carson," was the answer.

"Can you see Fred or Mik?"

From Todd: "I see a helmet on the other side of this wall segment."

Johnson: "Can you reach it?"

"Possibly. The section didn't cross the entire corridor."

Johnson: "OK, we're here. Move along the wall and get to the other side. Davis, follow him." A moment passed.

Todd: "I'm here. It's Fred."

Johnson: "Where's Mik? Scan the passage. Trovo, up the other way!"

"Nothing." "Zero."

Johnson: "I don't get it."

McDaniels spoke up. "We'd better get this wall off these two. Jack's barely breathing."

Johnson: "Right. Trovo, move along that wall until you're about midway of the fallen hunk. Davis, at the far corner. Mac, this corner. You three try to lift. We'll help if we can."

A moment passed for the bridge crew of the *Polaris*. Then Johnson came back on.

"Ready?"

Four answers came quickly.

"OK, lift!"

The straining of the three men was quite vocal. For seconds that seemed like hours, nothing issued from the radio except the strained breathing of the five security men. Then a small shout of triumph.

"Got him!" Johnson cried.

"Fred too!" Todd sounded. Then urgently. "Don't drop that wall! Mik's under there!"

"What?!"

Todd: "I saw a reflection from my light when I was pulling Fred's legs out!"

Johnson: "Well, we can't get him out. Let it down easy. Captain, I don't think a lifter would help."

"Johnson, get those injured out! Leave someone to watch and move out. Dralen has a crew waiting in *Darkstar*."

"Aye sir. Let's move! Trovo, stay."

Traynor spun to the communications console.

"Tell Dralen to take over *Friendship*'s responsibility. Also, inform him of Noverensky's accident. Then let De Gaulle know about the injured coming in."

Young Stuart's hands fairly flew across her board.

"Acknowledged, sir," she said after a moment. "Also, Lieutenant Nater reporting."

"Put him through."

"Captain, we've loaded the last of the group from the hangar deck. Also, I have two men with cutters about ten meters from the engineering section."

"Good work. Any problems?"

"None so far. Sir, is Mik in trouble?" Nater asked.

"He had an accident. A wall fell on him and part of his crew. Johnson got the others out, but Noverensky's under it completely. Dralen and his Vendrans are on their way. If anyone can get him out, they can. Just don't know if he's alive."

"Alex, is there anything I can do?" Nater asked softly. If the bridge crew noticed the use of the captain's proper name by Nater, they reacted as if nothing was out of place.

"Hal, you can't get there any faster than Dralen," Traynor replied in the same low tone. "We just have to wait. I don't like it either."

And wait the captain did, as *Friendship* arrived with its cargo. He waited as Trout radioed that he was bringing out the last load from *Moscow*'s sickbay and "B" deck lab. Traynor waited patiently, hardly hearing Nater's report that his men were through to the engineering section.

At last Dralen reported that his men were in position to lift the wall off Noverensky.

"Preparing to lift," Dralen reported. "Trovonski, grab him when we lift. Everyone, LIFT!"

The captain could picture in his mind's eye the eight Vendrans lifting, their massively muscled, compact bodies straining for every ounce of power they could provide. It might be tough, even for them, lifting it completely off the injured officer.

Trovonski: "I'm under the wall. About another ten centimeters and I've got him! . . . I'm pulling him out! . . . He's coming loose! , . . He's out!"

"Is he alive?" Traynor interrupted instantly.

"Aye, sir!" Trovonski radioed excitedly. Then his voice sobered. "Though just barely."

"Get him over here!" Traynor commanded quickly.

"Coming, sir!"

"Get moving! You too, Dralen!"

"Aye, sir," Dralen answered.

Traynor spun the chair and jumped out, heading for the exit.

"I'm on the hangar deck. Goldman, you have the con. If anything serious comes up, call me! Keep Nater and Dralen moving! Constant three-sixty by three-sixty at full sensor range!"

"Aye, sir," Goldman answered, stunned at the quick departure of the captain. When Traynor had left, he turned to navigator McMasters.

"Wonder what that's about?"

"Didnt' you read it?" she asked. Telepathically, she continued. *He blames himself for Noverensky's accident*, Maria informed Goldman.

Why? Goldman asked her mentally. *He couldn't have known the wall would fall. Of course there was an element of risk, but each person expects some danger when joining the Space Service. Especially security men.*

A good captain absorbs the responsibility for every action by his crew, was the telepathic reply. *The captain feels he should have pulled that crew out and let another crew handle it. They did have a lot of problems just getting to "B" deck.*

Why down to the hangar?

He's subconsciously trying to absolve the guilt he feels for Noverensky's accident. Being there might help.

Traynor hustled into the hangar deck and pushed his way to the operating tables. He inspected the wounded that had been treated; looked over the *Moscow* personnel that had remained unscathed. De Gaulle moved over to stand beside the captain.

"We're doing pretty good," De Gaulle said.

"Yeah, we are," Traynor agreed. "How's the *Moscow* crew doing?"

"So far, not so bad. Sixty-five transported. Lost two in transport, one on the table. Twenty-five criticals, twenty-one serious, the rest just had superficial injuries. We were under the gun for awhile, but on *Dawnstar*'s first return trip, two of *Moscow*'s surgeons came over. I put them to work immediately, even though they're about to drop."

"How's that girl Trout found in the corridor?"

"She's going to make it. By God, I did a good job on her. Another two or three minutes and she wouldn't be here, though."

Both men became silent, each with his own thoughts. The strain of putting the broken human bodies from *Moscow* had taken a telling effect on De Gaulle. He looked tired, though he'd only been on duty four and a half hours.

The worry over Noverensky's condition was evident on Traynor's face. The captain's normally bright and pleasant disposition was absent, replaced by a much more solemn expression. It was plain to all around that Traynor was interested only in the injured man coming in on the next LC.

Marge Upshaw joined the two. She saluted the captain, then spoke to De Gaulle.

"Marchetti says Carson's pretty bad, but if there are no complications, he should recover completely. Louise, 'ah, Doctor Malvin, checked Peterson and didn't bother with surgery. It seems Peterson just got conked on the head, then pinned under the wall. Maybe a fractured rib or so." The captain winced in sympathy, knowing how painful rib injuries could be. "But nothing serious. To tell the truth," Marge continued, lowering her voice. "Louise was about to have a fit about wasting her time, until she noticed he was a *Polaris* crewman." De Gaulle roared with laughter. Even Traynor, worried as he was, had to smile.

"I can picture that plainly," De Gaulle laughed to Traynor. "You have to see something like that to get the full effect. Louise Malvin is the most fun to watch when she's upset of anyone I've ever known."

"Tell the young lady that her sentiments are commendable," Traynor told the head nurse. As he spoke to Marge Upshaw, the captain took the opportunity to observe firsthand the person who had captured De Gaulle's attention so quickly.

She was a tall woman, easily ten centimeters taller than the captain. Blonde hair was cut short, yet stylish, trimmed to reveal her ears. She had an open face, with a bright, intelligent, efficient air about her. Her figure was flawless in the classic statuesqueness of the ancient Greek stone carvings. Marge wore the traditional woman's uniform of the Space Service: a sleeveless tunic from neck to just below the waist, worn with either slacks or a skirt. Marge wore the skirt, accentuating her long and shapely legs. As with the others on duty, she wore work blues.

"*Dawnstar* arriving with casualties," a medical technician called, rushing to where the landing craft was being raised from its docking bay. Several others also hurried to the newly arrived aircraft.

"Unless there's a super critical, keep my table clear," De Gaulle requested, as Marge made to leave.

"For Noverensky?" she asked. He nodded. She hurried off, and quickly made her presence known among the youngsters unloading the injured.

"*Darkstar*, Captain," Myra Shanesey's voice sounded.

Traynor glanced around to see the small ship rising on its docking platform. He rushed over and leaped to the platform before it had reached deck level. He was standing below the hatch when it opened and the auto-ladder engaged. When the ladder was in place, Traynor rushed up and looked in. Trovonski was lifting Noverensky's broken body.

"Is he alive?"

"Barely," Trovonski replied. "Been floating in and out of consciousness since we took him out." Between the two, they were able to carry the injured man down the ladder.

"Marc!" yelled Traynor. "Over here!"

"Get him here, Alex!" De Gaulle yelled back. "Marge, assist!"

Slowly, careful not to move the man any more than necessary, Traynor and Trovonski crossed the hangar to where Marc De Gaulle, Marge Upshaw, and Hildy Bennett were waiting beside the operating table. The two laid the man on the table. De Gaulle took charge instantly.

"Hildy, cut him out of that suit! Marge, the electro-cardio stimulator! Also, an intra-trachea tube! Looks like we'll have to open him up. Alex, get out of here! I'll let you know! Someone check the prox-sterilizer!"

Traynor moved away, sliding over to the far wall to stand by himself and watch the crew of the *Polaris* handle their duties. They moved with amazing cool and control, going about their duties like a veteran crew, instead of the rookies most were. The captain was proud of his crew, even if certain members were royal pains in the neck. The crew obeyed orders and pulled together.

However, Traynor thought uncomfortably, the members of the crew most likely to cause problems weren't in the hangar. Except Jenkins, of course, but he was too busy to cause problems.

A young man, wearing the uniform of the *Moscow*, with Major's stripes and the science insignia, crossed over to where Traynor stood.

"Sir," he began, saluting. "I'm Major Keloff Tronston, science officer of *Moscow*. I've been doing some checking, and of the survivors not in critical condition, I seem to be senior."

"Yes, Major?" Traynor questioned.

"I'd like to thank you for rescuing what's left of the crew."

"You can thank me by telling me what happened." Traynor replied quickly, a bite in his voice. He relented quickly, seeing the strain the man was under already. Not much more than a kid, Traynor thought. Oberonite, he decided. Well, they mature young.

Taken aback by the tone of the captain to his conciliatory remarks, Tronston paused to regain his composure. Traynor smiled encouragingly, allowing the young man to sigh with relief.

"Well, sir, we were on a routine patrol. Sensors on half-range, constant three-sixty three-sixty." The man paused to carefully consider what he was saying. "We were at sub-light. There was a minor malfunction in the neutronium drive. Nothing serious, but the chief engineer wanted to fix it.

"All of a sudden, an enemy ship flashed onto the sensor plates. We got our screens up, but it came in and blasted away. We went at it for over six hours!"

"Why didn't you radio for help?"

"We didn't think we'd need it. And we couldn't run because the chief engineer had broken down the neutronium-drive components and wasn't able to get them together during the battle."

"The enemy ship could have called for help," Traynor pointed out.

"Colonel Kilter reasoned that if they were alone, they would stay alone. He is, was, a student of the enemy's battle tactics. From reports of previous battles he has, ah, had, formed a theory concerning their tactics. The enemy does not seem to reinforce its battle fleets. Nowhere in any of the reports has there ever been evidence of enemy reinforcements arriving on the scene of a battle. Apparently the enemy sends ships to do a job, and if they can't, they run."

"An interesting theory," Traynor said thoughtfully. There could be something to this theory. He would have to check out the computer records. However, thought Traynor, Kilter might not have called because of the foolish pride that is part of an Oberonite's breeding. The USR's only natural soldiers were these descendants of the military survivors of Earth's World War III. Perhaps the theory Kilter had developed about the enemy could be applied with equal success when referring to Kilter's own people.

"At approximately the same time, both our and the enemy's shields overloaded. We were hit primarily with disruptors. Some laser fire. We hit them with everything we had. Disruptors and lasers, all banks. I really think they got the worst of it."

"If you got the better of that exchange, then that ship must be completely gutted," Traynor decided. "Thank you, Major. We'll do our best for your crew. Shouldn't be long before we get underway for OS 28."

"Thank you, sir," Tronston answered, saluting.

For another twenty minutes Traynor remained on the hangar deck. He spent the time wandering from the medical area to Myra Shanesey's launch controls. Commander Shanesey ran him away from the control area when he began questioning her launch and docking procedure. Traynor did not argue, or use his authority as captain, realizing that she was the expert on the hangar deck. Also, Traynor had learned through the ship's grapevine that arguing with Myra Shanesey was like arguing with a wall. She was known to have challenged the authority of admirals when she had reason. And she was renowned for winning more than she lost.

The captain was leaving the hangar deck when *Discovery* returned for the last time. By the time Traynor had made his way slowly to the bridge, *Friendship* was preparing to dock with *Polaris*. He took the command chair quietly and gazed at the screen, which was dominated by the image of *Moscow*.

"*Friendship* aboard, sir," Lieutenant Stuart reported.

"Sensor scan of *Moscow*," Traynor commanded.

"Begging your pardon, sir." Danart N'goto, who had returned to his position as duty science officer, spoke up. "But we scanned the ship and found all life forms when we arrived in this sector."

"Colonel N'goto, scan the *Moscow*," Traynor again ordered, through clenched teeth, his gaze fixed on the USR ship. The others on the bridge were silent.

"But, sir . . ." N'goto began. Stuart gasped. To question a direct order from a Fleet captain was not even in her realm of thought.

Slowly Traynor turned to the science station. His eyes flashed fire as his gaze bore into the black. Quickly N'goto spun and began working the controls at his station. He looked into the small computer visiscreen for the results, then turned back to the captain. Traynor was still staring at him with blazing eyes. N'goto knew the captain was not to be trifled with at this moment.

"Sensor report negative, sir," N'goto quickly recited the results. "No life forms aboard *Moscow*."

"Thank you, Mr. N'goto," Traynor said, turning forward. "Mr. Torval, put a tractor on *Moscow*. Also, put one on that other ship. Miss McMasters, plot a course to Station Twenty-Eight. Mr. Goldman, when Torval and Miss McMasters are ready, implement at cruise speed. Mr. N'goto, constant three-sixty by three-sixty. Once under way, Lieutenant Stuart, you may bring the ship off red alert, but remain on yellow alert."

"Aye, sir," came a chorus of replies.

"Tractors on," Lieutenant Torval called.

"Course prepared," Maria McMasters sung out.

"Implementing," came from Goldman.

"Sensors operational, full range," N'goto added softly.

And over their voices, Traynor could hear Lieutenant Stuart, shipwide, calling off the red alert, but keeping *Polaris* on yellow alert.

Polaris's return to Kappa Barnard was uneventful. The trip took over two and a half hours, arriving within sensor range of the "Rock" almost seven hours after departing to answer *Moscow's* distress signal.

Captain Traynor went off duty at 2000 hours RST (Republic Standard Time), leaving the job of transferring the rescued crew of *Moscow* from *Polaris* to OS 28, to his relief officer, Commander Robert Parker.

Commanders Goldman and McMasters were relieved at 2000 hours also. They joined the captain in the elevator, headed for the "C" deck lounge to celebrate *Polaris*' successful mission. They invited the captain to join them.

"No," Traynor replied as they moved swiftly through the ship in the elevator. "I don't feel much like celebrating right now."

Goldman started to speak, but Maria McMasters gripped his arm tightly, silencing him instantly.

"We understand, Captain," she said.

"Do you?" Traynor asked. He then remembered the heritage of the woman to whom he was speaking. "Perhaps you do," he acknowledged.

They separated on "C" deck, the two Iapetans heading for the lounge while Traynor continued to his cabin. The young couple stepped through the automatic doors of the lounge and were instantly assailed by the deafening roar of a huge party going on. It seemed as if every off-duty crew member was there, celebrating. From a corner to their left came a loud yell with an Ioan accent.

"Bring yourselves over this way!" Shawn O'Leery sang out. McMasters and Goldman pushed their way through the crowded room to join O'Leery and his party. Their addition made the number seventeen seated at the two long tables, which had been pulled together for the occasion.

"What'll ye be drinkin', folks?" O'Leery continued loudly.

"Shawn O'Leery, must you be so loud?" Major Marge Upshaw reprimanded the engineer. "No one can hold a decent conversation with you around."

"That's what I've been telling him for quite a while now," Myra Shanesey told the group. "Does he listen to me?"

"Come now, me darlin's, this is a time for celebratin'," O'Leery countered. "And meself, I've never been to a celebration where there wasn't noise. Am I right?" A chorus of "ayes" drowned him out.

Everyone began talking at once, laughing and carrying on, as the drinks flowed liberally. Besides the two Iapetans, Shanesey, O'Leery, and Upshaw, crowded at the tables were Mark Carter, Hal Nater, and Peter Trout of security, Kran and Vlres from communications, and Erica LeMay from engineering. Marc De

Gaulle had finished up with Noverensky, successfully, and tagged along. Jay Farnsworth and David Emerson had accompanied Angela Martin and Emily Dawson, a Europan who piloted *Dawnstar*. Carol Ann Jorgenson, pilot of *Providence*, sat next to Peter Trout, engaged in a highly animated discussion.

"Where's the Captain?" De Gaulle asked Goldman when he could finally work his way over to engage the young pilot.

"His cabin, I guess," Goldman replied. "Maria knows more. We asked him to join us, but he said he didn't feel like it."

"Let's move down and talk with Maria," De Gaulle suggested. They spotted Maria and Major Kran at the head of the table, deeply involved in a conversation with Erica LeMay. The two men pushed their way toward the women.

"You know, he was on top of everything at once," Peter Trout was saying as De Gaulle and Goldman pushed past. "I could hear him giving instructions to the other crews, you know, busy with what they were doing. All of a sudden he jumps in and tells me one of my guys has a problem, or is about to lose it. I had a couple of youngsters with me, and they got a little shaky seeing that mess on the *Moscow*. But just about the time one's losing it, the captain alerts me and I cool 'im down."

"Captain Hawkins wouldn't have been as alert," Mark Carter spoke up. "And you know Nelson couldn't have handled it." He added disgustedly.

Goldman stopped to speak.

"You should have heard him handle Johnson when Noverensky lost contact. I thought that kid was going to go over the edge. I think I would have, and I've been around awhile. It's the kids first action. But Captain Traynor just told him exactly what to do. Cool and calm."

"It's a way he's got about him," Hal Nater noted. "You're calm because he's calm. He knows you can do the job, and that gives you the confidence to do it."

"Really, Hal, philosophy from you?" Trout laughed.

"I have been known to spout a few words of wisdom in my times," Nater replied, feigning indignation.

"Robert, let's move on up," De Gaulle suggested again. He was looking at the threesome of LeMay, McMasters, and Kran, talking quietly together. The two men finally reached the head of the table as Erica jumped up and made a quick exit from the lounge.

"Where's she headed?" De Gaulle asked.

"Really, Major De Gaulle," Kran replied indignantly. "Must everyone on board this ship account to the ship's doctor at every moment of the day?"

"No, uh, that is, I didn't mean to pry," De Gaulle sputtered. So flustered was he that he did not see the slight wink Maria McMasters gave Goldman, nor the knowing smile that crept to his lips.

Hal Nater rose to his feet, his two-meter-plus frame striking an imposing figure. He raised his glass.

"May I have your attention?" he asked loudly.

"Knock it off!" Mark Carter boomed. The group came to an abrupt silence.

"Thank you," Nater smiled. "And thank you, Commander Carter."

"My pleasure," Carter replied sarcastically.

"A toast, ladies and gentlemen, to Alex Traynor." He paused. "The Captain."

"The Captain!" the others echoed, lifting their glasses.

In another part of the ship, another meeting was

also in progress. In Carl Nelson's quarters, eight officers were deep in discussion. None of these crew members would have echoed Nater's sentiments.

Nelson was still highly disturbed over the incident on the bridge of the *Polaris*, as were Victoria Spencer and Danart N'goto. Ben Peters sat with his perpetual hangdog expression, awaiting the outcome of the meeting. Corensky sat boredly listening to the conversation. His views were already known to those gathered. Corensky favored an immediate takeover by the loyal Earthers on *Polaris*. Francis Jenkins backed Corensky. The remaining two, Commander Reg Dickson, a scientist and the first to feel the long arm of Traynor's presence when relieved of the main computer overhaul, and Millie Makem, a pilot, were listening intently to Nelson.

"No man makes a fool of me!" Nelson stormed. "And especially not in front of outworlders! He humiliated me in front of those 'people'!" He used the word in a highly derogatory tone. "Relieving me of duty. Me! There's no way I'm going to let up on him now."

"I still say declare him unfit for command and take over. We have enough people to carry it out," Corensky insisted loudly.

"We can't Vlad," N'goto spoke up. All eyes turned to him. "Not according to regulations, at least," he added quickly.

"Th-that's right," Peters stuttered. "Regulation four-seven-one."

"Which says?" Corensky demanded.

"Which says, Vlad, as you well know, that along with the Exec, the science officer, and the chief engineer, on a Centurion-class ship, the chief surgeon and the communications officer must be in on the decision. And it must be a unanimous decision," Nelson explained bitterly. "You don't think the doctor or that Pronethan would agree, now do you?"

"We could make them agree," Corensky said slowly.

"And be imprisoned and tried for mutiny," Spencer finished for him. "I, for one, don't want to end up in a penal settlement."

"I don't think we could make them anyway," Nelson added.

"You know. it's strange how Traynor was prepared to squelch the rumors we started about him and the Vendrans so quickly," Jenkins mentioned to no one in particular.

"There's no telling what else he knows," Nelson added. "However, we do have a black mark against him. Book three, Section six, Paragraph one of the Space Service Regulations, and I quote: 'Under battle alert conditions, the senior officer of each department (excluding medical) shall be on the bridge, that the captain may benefit from their knowledge."

"That's not enough to do anything," Commander Makem was quick to point out. "It's happened on board other ships I've been on."

"Good point, Millie," Nelson agreed. "In itself, the three-six-one is not enough. Couple it with the humiliation suffered by the senior officers, along with the loss of dignity to the executive officer at being relieved of duty when complying with regulations, and you have a large mark against Traynor. Also, you might remember the incident at Station Fifteen. We went into battle against the direct orders of Traynor's superior officer, in this case, Rear Admiral Antonozzi."

"Sounds like you have enough to go before a board now, Carl," Jenkins observed, smiling.

"Oh, I have quite a bit, but nothing big," Nelson replied. "I don't have a kicker. Something that would really be heavy stuff."

"Where does that leave us?" Makem asked. "You do realize that we're losing our popularity with the Earthers in the crew?"

"No, I didn't," Nelson answered, amazed. "Who?"

"Angele Martin," Makem answered, adding sarcastically, "Traynor's private pilot."

"I never considered her in the first place," Nelson said grimly. "Who else?"

"Mercy Thompson."

"Med tech, isn't she?" Jenkins asked.

"Right," was the answer.

"I'll check on it," Jenkins volunteered.

"Next," Makem continued. "Beth Maxwell."

"Beth?" Spencer asked, surprised.

"That's right," Makem answered. "And most of the Lunarites that we had persuaded to our way of thinking."

"I didn't realize we were having this big a defection," Nelson said. "We'd better get moving. Start playing up Traynor's bad points when you talk to the loyal followers. Try to bring back those that have deserted us. Use whatever means available."

"Any means?" Corensky asked, grinning evilly.

"Yes."

The automatic door slid open.

"Captain," Erica LeMay called out. "Alex, are you here?" She stepped through the door, then jumped, startled, as the door slid shut behind her.

"Wha. . .who's there?" Traynor appeared at the entrance to his sleeping quarters, wearing just trousers, his hair disheveled. He noticed the girl standing across the room.

"Something I can do for you, Erica?" he asked,

moving slowly to the desk and taking a seat. "I do hope you will forgive my appearance. I wasn't expecting anyone."

"Yes, of course," she said, passing it over quickly. "I came to tell you that Marc De Gaulle was successful with Noverensky. If there are no complications, Noverensky should recover with no effects." Traynor's spirits lifted visibly for a moment, then returned to their former low. "Also," Erica continued. "I came to find out why you weren't celebrating such a successful mission."

"Thank you for worrying, Major," Traynor sighed. "But I don't really feel like celebrating."

"Alex, what's wrong?" Erica demanded, crossing the room and dropping into a chair. "I was talking to Kran and McMasters. They believe that you are blaming yourself for Noverensky's accident."

"Well, whose fault is it?!" Traynor shouted, jumping up and stalking into the back area. "Who else would you blame?"

Erica followed him into the back.

"Why is it your fault?!" she answered him in like tones. "You weren't there!"

She paused, letting what she had said sink in. It gave her a chance to glance around the room. She admired the captain's fine, yet simple, taste. Two small landscapes hung on the wall over the bunk. Erica assumed they were of Earth. Several books, real books, were on a stand beside the bunk, which was somewhat mussed.

"I saw it coming! Accident after accident! I knew something was going to happen; someone was going to get hurt! I could've prevented it. I had another crew standing by. All I had to do was tell him to come back. That's all! Dralen, with his fresh approach, might not have had an accident."

"Alex, you couldn't have known about that wall," Erica pointed out quickly. "Besides, you know the pride inherent in security men. If you had pulled Noverensky, he would have lost face among his friends and peers. Right now he's something of a hero. May I sit down?"

"Sure. If he'd been killed, would that help his pride?"

She pulled a seat over by the bunk, where Traynor sat. "It's one of those 'damned if you do, damned if you don't' situations," she replied.

Traynor managed a weak smile.

"Just full of those wonderful sayings, aren't you?" he said.

"That's right," she laughed, then sobered. "But there's something else, isn't there? Tell me Alex. What's the real problem?"

"The real problem," Traynor echoed her. He dropped his head to think, his hands gripping the edge of the bed tightly. Several moments passed quietly, as Traynor sat thinking, and Erica waited expectantly.

"It's a long way," he finally began. "From commanding a planetary outpost, or one of the smaller class ships, to the command chair of *Polaris*. This ship is one of the most powerful creations of mankind. Think of the people depending on this ship, and what could happen if something went wrong. And all this power, this responsibility, rests on one person's shoulders. Me.

"I do my best. God knows I try. Carry out orders, trying to do the best for the crew at all times. Yet, no matter what I do, I have a nagging doubt in my mind that it could be wrong. I just don't know if I'm ready for this."

"You've done a fine job so far," Erica pointed out.

"Have I?" Traynor asked. "Perhaps. I have tried. When every order you give is questioned, though, you begin to wonder if maybve someone knows more than you."

"That could be true in other cases," Erica agreed. "But not in yours. You've been too worried about what other people think. Remember, you're the captain. You can't let others change that. To paraphrase a certain person we both know: 'If you let their rantings and ravings get to you, you'll crack! And, Alex Traynor, I won't have that! When they start, fight back!' You're the captain! Make sure they know it!"

"You won't have it?" he asked smiling.

She returned his smile.

"That's right, Alex," she said softly. "I won't have it."

0900 hours the next working day, Carl Nelson hit the announce button on the entrance controls of Captain Traynor's cabin door. The automatic door slid open, revealing Traynor seated at his desk.

"Come in, Colonel," Traynor said quietly. Nelson entered and stood at attention.

"I'll come right to the point, Colonel," Traynor began. "Your behavior since my arrival aboard *Polaris* has been disgraceful." Nelson started to speak, but Traynor silenced him with a wave of his hand. "You have been disrespectful to me, your commanding officer. You have berated and criticized other officers on board this ship without reason. You attempt to countermand my orders. You attempt to demoralize the crew and disrupt the effectiveness of this ship.

"I won't have it! I realize you feel that you were passed over when I was given command and, until the incident yesterday, I was allowing for this fact. However, you must remember that I am the captain, and I give the orders on this ship! If that doesn't suit you, I can have you transferred."

"No thank you, sir," Nelson replied meekly. He was quite unprepared for the captain's remarks.

"Nelson, this is my ship. MY ship!" Traynor stressed. "I hope I've made myself clear, both yesterday and today. . ."

"Yes sir, you did," Nelson replied.

"Very good, Colonel," Traynor said. "That's all. Dismissed."

Nelson turned on his heel and exited.

"Little strong, weren't you?" Erica LeMay asked, as she entered from the private quarters. She straightened her work tunic.

"Who was it saying I should fight back; let them know who's boss?"

"I know," she smiled. "But I didn't think you'd start so quickly."

"It's about time I put him in his place," answered Traynor. "Dammit Erica, I'm the captain! He's got to come to terms with that or get out!"

"Or get rid of you," Erica added.

"We'll come to that when it gets here," he told her, standing up. He gave the girl a quick kiss on the cheek, then hurried into the other room. She followed, smiling to herself.

V

"Standard orbit established, sir," Commander Robert Goldman called out.

"Message from the planet Larandra," Lieutenant Mary Stuart spoke up. " 'To those aboard the USR *Polaris*, Welcome!' "

"Message for the planet Larandra," Traynor answered. "To the people of Larandra from the USR *Polaris*: Thank you, and our congratulations."

Polaris had entered orbit around Larandra, known on the navigation charts as Eta Barnard, on a diplomatic mission for the Interplanetary Council of the USR. In the two weeks since the successful rescue of the disabled *Moscow*, much had happened in the politics of the Republic.

In the Interplanetary Council, the coalition of Barnard planets had forced a showdown vote on Eta Barnard's petition for independence. By a vote of thirteen to seven, the exact number of votes needed, Eta Barnard was granted its independence as the free planet of Larandra. A second vote, for the purpose of admitting Larandra to the IC, ended in favor of Larandra by a vote of seventeen to three, Osiris and Isis of the Sirius star system, along with Titania and the Fleet Command changing sides on the second vote, leaving only Earth, Lunar, and Titan to vote against the measure.

Also passed by a vote of seventeen to three was a

measure to be officially represented at the ceremonies marking the declaration of independence of Larandra. Their representative would be a USR Space Service Ship's Captain. The Larandran government was agreeable to IC representation, with the provision that they, the Larandrans, would be allowed to choose the captain to act as USR representative. The captain chosen was Alexander Traynor of *Polaris*.

Polaris was a highly talked-about ship in the meantime. The Space Service had commended Traynor and the crew of *Polaris* on successfully rescuing not only the surviving crew members of *Moscow*, but *Moscow* itself; and on successfully returning with what was left of the enemy craft. *Polaris*'s prize marked the first time in the long history of the space war that an enemy ship had been captured semi-intact by a Republic ship. The enemy ship was towed to Mimnon base to be studied by scientists to determine as much as possible about the enemy.

Polaris, upon receiving its orders, made its way speedily to the planet. Traynor's orders involved his ship in patrol around Larandra for twelve to fourteen days. He received permission to allow his crew to go ashore for rest and recreation. The crew would be allowed on Larandra in groups of fifty, with forty-eight hour passes. The first crew, selected by the captain, consisted of twenty-six crew people chosen to participate in the ceremonies. They would also be allowed their forty-eight hours of R and R.

Aboard *Polaris*, routine had become the order of business during the two eventful weeks. Morale though, had taken a turn upwards against the ever constant pressure of the Earth First party members. One of the major causes of the upswing, along with the success of *Polaris*'s first mission under its new captain, was rumor passing through the ship of the relationship developing between the captain and Erica LeMay: a relationship neither they, nor anyone close to them, would confirm.

"The following personnel assemble on the hangar deck for shore leave," Mary Stuart announced throughout the ship. "Majors Bennet, Kran, and LeMay. Commanders Beaumont, Dickson, Feather, Goldman, Makem, Maxwell, McMasters, O'Casey, O'Leery, Shanesey, and Vlres. Lieutenants Farnsworth, Kevin Johnson, Carol Ann Jorgenson, Lornton,Martin, Millerand, Nater, Clancy O'Hanrahan, Peterson, Mercy Thompson, and Trout."

"Let's go, Commanders," Traynor snapped to his navigator and pilot. Goldman and Maria McMasters joined him at the elevator door. Their relief crew quickly filled the vacant seats. Carl Nelson rose from his Exec console to assume the command chair.

"You have command, Colonel," Traynor said quickly. "Keep her in synchronized orbit above Collova. The shore party will be within the Collova city limits the entire leave. Any problems, get me or Majors Kran or LeMay on the command frequency. Then issue an alert, subject to an all call. Other then that, see you in two days. " Nelson saluted stiffly.

On the hangar deck the other members of the landing party, to the number of twenty-three, had already gathered. Each officer wore dress blues and carried a small clothing bag, which contained the individual's dress whites, along with other personal items. The group was excitedly discussing the prospective shore leave when Traynor, Goldman, and McMasters arrived. The group came to attention.

"At ease," Traynor called. He looked for and caught the eye of Erica LeMay. She nodded and motioned to the two bags at her feet, which he assumed were his and hers. McMasters and Goldman went to stand beside Angela Martin and Jay Farnsworth, who had seen to it the two Iapetans' overnight bags had arrived on the deck.

"All right, ladies and gentlemen, let's go over the basics again," Traynor began.

"Again?" someone groaned. Laughter came from the back.

"Yes, again," Traynor grinned. "Collova is the capital of Larandra. Make sure you call the planet Larandra in any public place. Remember, your pass is for forty-eight hours, not two days. The planetary rotation is thirty standard hours. Don't lose track. Remember also that the planet has a gravity of slightly more than one Earth gravity. Shouldn't be much trouble, but be advised.

"Stay in groupos of at least two, preferably four or more. Do not leave the city limits, though as big as Collova reportedly is, I'll be surprised if anyone finds the city limits.

"If there is an 'all call,' drop whatever you're doing and beat it to the space port immediately!"

"Drop it immediately?" Fred Peterson called out. "Captain, what if you're not in position to drop everything?"

"You'll just have to, Lieutenant," Traynor said, adding, "Tell her you love her. She'll understand." The men from security, six in all, roared with laughter. Several ladies blushed.

"Try to have a good time," Traynor continued. "Do avoid any problems with the locals! I don't want to have to bail anyone out of the local jail. If you have any trouble, use your communicators.

"Other then that, let's go!"

A chorus of sarcastic amens greeted his final remark. The group then made to board *Discovery*. Traynor joined Erica, Hal Nater, and Hildy Bennett, waiting their turn to board. He relieved the Europan girl of his bag.

"Think that last talk was well received?" Traynor asked, laughing.

"Not really," Nater replied, also laughing. "Was it necessary?"

"You know it was, Hal Nater," Erica LeMay defended the captain. "You may be an old hand at going on shore leave, but what about the youngsters? What about Martin? O'Hanrahan? Johnson? Think they will remember if it isn't drilled into their heads?"

"Hey, hold on, Erica. I was just joking," Nater replied defensively.

"It's OK, Erica," Traynor laughed. "Hal understands my way of thinking." To Nater he explained. "Erica's a bit defensive about criticism towards yours truly. Sometimes she doesn't recognize friend from foe."

"You don't have to defend me," Erica interrupted indignantly. Then she smiled. "But you are right. Sorry, Hal."

"Don't apologize to him," Hildy Bennett insisted quickly. "He deserves a good tongue-lashing," she added severely. Then, laughing, she finished. "Here again you've opened your mouth once to often, Hal Nater."

The ride to the planet surface was uneventful. They arrived at the large spaceport to be received by thousands of celebrating Larandrans. Each *Polaris* crew member was greeted by a teenage girl in a long flowing white gown with flowers attractively arranged in her hair. The girls placed a small red flower behind the right ear of each Space Service member, then escorted them to a huge raised platform erected for the welcoming ceremonies.

Traynor mounted the platform last. His crew had been led to seats on the dias while his escort led him forward, where Larandran dignitaries waited, talking among themselves. The leader turned to receive *Polaris*'s captain and Traynor instantly recognized the man's face from over two months earlier. Akamel Drakar!

"Captain Traynor." Drakar hurried his huge bulk forward. It's so good to see you again." Traynor shook the man's hand, smiling.

"It's good to see you again, sir," he replied. "I was wondering how *Polaris*, with a relatively new captain, rated an honor such as this."

"When the Interplanetary Council informed Larandra of their wishes concerning the use of a ship's captain as their representative to the celebration, I immediately thought of you," Drakar explained.

"I'm honored you remember me, and I thank you, for myself and my crew, for the honor of being allowed to participate in this occasion," Traynor smiled. "Excuse me sir, but exactly how should my crew and myself address you? Will Ambassador Drakar be acceptable?"

"It would have been, two months ago," Drakar replied. "But now I hold a different position."

"Really, sir?"

"In the elections of a week ago, held after receiving word that we had been voted into the Interplanetary Council," Drakar paused for effect. "I was selected Vice-Premier."

"My congratulations!" Traynor exclaimed.

An aide spoke to Drakar. He replied in a hushed tone, then turned back to the captain.

"The head of the People's House will be joining us in a moment. Then we will begin," Drakar explained. "This opening address will be broadcast across the continent, and to the outlands on the other continents."

"I wish you hadn't told me that," Traynor grimaced. "I'm nervous enough as it is."

"Nonsense, my boy," laughed Drakar. "Tomorrow's address should be the one to worry about. We've arranged radio links with the ruling bodies of the governments of the United Space Republic. The official declaration of independence of Larandra by the Premier will be seen throughout the Republic.

"Ah, here comes the Speaker of the People's House, Dratvin Pasteur," Drakar announced. Then he remembered the clash between Traynor and Pasteur. "Oh my, I do hope you and Dratvin will not have words."

"Sir, for myself and my people, I assure you we will do our best, and myself especially, to keep anything from happening during the festivities." Traynor's words seemed to relieve the worried politician.

"Good day Captain Traynor," Dratvin Pasteur coldly addressed *Polaris*'s commander.

"A good day to you, Mr. Speaker," Traynor replied formally.

"Shall we begin, gentlemen?" an aide interrupted. "If you will take your seats." He motioned to the three chairs placed at the front of the dais. Traynor was escorted to a seat. Dratvin Pasteur took a seat, and Drakar settled his bulk into the seat separating the two men.

The aide stepped to the microphone of the micro-radio transmitter and waved his hands to silence the huge crowd gathered before the platform.

"Friends, Larandrans, honored guests. Today marks the first day of celebration for the independence of our world!" A loud cheer rose from the mass before the speaker. "To begin the festivities officially," the aide continued, "The Vice-Premier!"

The crowd roared its approval as Drakar stood. The Vice-Premier of Larandra stepped forward, acknowledging the cheers of the gathered throng. Once at the microphone, he waved for silence.

"Fellow citizens of Larandra," Drakar began. "Greetings. Today, the third day of the month of Solstice on Larandra, corresponding with the seventh of May, in the year 2458 of the Republic's calendar, we are gathered together in a celebration of the independence of our world.

"Tomorrow's festivities will mark the official granting of independence of our world by the United States Republic. At that time we will also be formally inducted into the Interplanetary Council.

"To do those honors, representing the United Space Republic, the Interplanetary Council, and the Space Service, is the commander of the Fleet heavy cruiser *Polaris*, Captain Alexander Traynor!" Traynor stood, waving to the people. They responded with cheers, though not quite the deafening roar that Vice-Premier Drakar had received.

At the proper moment, Traynor stepped to the microphone. The crowd grew respectfully quiet.

"People of Larandra," Traynor said. "On behalf of the United Space Republic, the Interplanetary Council, the Space Service, the men and women of *Polaris*, and myself, congratulations! Welcome to the Republic!" The crowd cheered happily for several moments in response. Traynor waved again and sat down.

"Thank you Captain Traynor," Drakar spoke gratefully into the microphone. "To answer, for the people of Larandra, is the Speaker of the People's House, Dratvin Pasteur!" Pasteur stepped to the microphone, to the jubilant cheers of the excited crowd.

"Thank you my friends," he said to the crowd. "Thank you Mr. Vice-Premier. A welcome to Captain Traynor and the crew of *Polaris* from the people of Larandra." Pasteur addressed Traynor. The captain nodded his head in acceptance of the salutation.

"From the people of Larandra to the United Space Republic, congratulations on finally reaching the only sensible decision available to you. Larandra is now a planet, recognized as an independent entity, with its own government and way of life!" Pasteur's words added to the emotional frenzy of the crowd. Larandran governmental police moved the excited people, hoping against hope to keep them under control.

"No longer are we under the control of the Interplanetary Council, subject to the whims of the controlling factions of that body!"

"That guy's doing a good job of stirring these people up," Kevin Johnson remarked to the man next to him, Rene Millerand. "Did you see the way he glared meaningfully at the Captain when he brought up that part about 'whims of the controlling factions' of the IC?"

"He doesn't appear to like the Captain," Millerand agreed. "Did you see the look he gave Captain Traynor when they first met? Boy, if looks could kill, the Captain would be dead and buried by now. Wonder what's with that guy?"

"It has been a long fight, my friends," continued Pasteur. "Long and hard, battling against people and planetary political ideologies which fear the admittance of new planets to the freedoms they themselves enjoy. Granting independence to the young planets brings about a loss in power and prestige to the older planets.

"But, fellow Larandrans, we have done it! We are now full-fledged citizens of the Republic! Be proud of your new position, and know that at all times your government will be struggling in your best interest, while we fight in the Interplanetary Council for the good of the Republic. Congratulations, Larandrans!" The crowd noise became deafening. Pasteur's flowery words of Larandran greatness worked the crowd into a fevered pitch.

As the crowd pushed forward, Traynor and his crew were escorted to a waiting bus, which carried them to the hotel prepared for the visitors. The bus skimmed across the surface on a Z-grav cushion, driven by one small jet. It passed out of the spaceport and into the city proper, giving the newcomers a look at the impressive city that was Collova, Larandra's capital. Over 15 million of the 950 million inhabitants of Larandra lived in Collova.

Huge buildings rose from either side of the avenue. Office buildings and apartment complexes rose over a hundred and fifty stories. Monstrous stores that took up an entire city block attracted the eyes of *Polaris*'s crew.

The bus stopped in front of one of the huge buildings. Traynor led his people out and into the lobby of the Hotel Starlight, the hotel set aside for visiting dignitaries. The broad, open room that was the lobby, was decorated in white and various shades of blue. The carpet was a plush, deep-blue pile of a material manufactured on Drina. The blue carpet was contrasted by the white walls and columns, of a material similar to marble, but found only on Larandra.

The *Polaris* personnel were taken up to their rooms, an entire wing reserved on the fortieth floor of the hotel: twenty-six single rooms for the twenty-six officers of the Space Service.

The rooms were magnificent. They were actually three rooms: living area, private bedroom, and refresher unit. There was a video-viewer, a vidiphone, and the double bed was a Z-grav neutralized contraption that allowed the person, or persons, using it the feeling of total weightlessness. The floors, as in the lobby and the halls, were carpeted in the same plush pile, tastefully coordinated to match the color scheme of the individual rooms. A huge, balconied, plastiglass door filled one wall of the bedroom, curtained in color-coordinated material.

A door in the wall of the living area connected Traynor's room with the room next door. The captain knocked on the connecting door, curious to discover who was in the adjacent room. He pulled his door open and the second door swung open to reveal the flashing eyes and broad smile of Erica LeMay.

"Surprise!" she laughed.

"Pleasantly, of course," he assured her, smiling.

"Hal Nater had this room, but he and I traded," she explained. "My room was connected to Hildy Bennett." She gave him a sly wink.

"I see."

"Hildy and I thought it would be best," she added.

"No problem," grinned Traynor. "How someone spends their R and R is their own business." There was a knock at Traynor's door. Opening it revealed Hal Nater and Hildy Bennett. Major Bennett bounced eagerly in.

"Hello, Captain," she smiled. She saw the connecting doors opened and giggled. "I might have expected this." Bennett stepped over to the doors to stand beside Erica.

"Tell me, miss, has this young man made any compromising suggestions," asked Bennett, giggling.

"No, he hasn't," replied Erica, a twinkle in her eye. "And I'm tired of waiting." The four laughed.

"Is everyone settled in?" Traynor asked.

"Aye, sir," nodded Nater. "In fact, several have already left for. . .I believe they went shopping."

"Already? Who?"

"Beaumont, Feather, Maxwell, O'Casey, Thompson, and Kevin Johnson." Nater rattled off the names. "I sent Johnson because a group like that could attract some unwarranted attention."

"Poor Johnson," sympathized Erica. "I imagine

those girls will hit every store in Collova." She winced, thinking about Johnson being dragged along by the women.

"Not to worry," laughed Hildy. "Johnson is head over heels for Mercy Thompson, and she has a huge crush on him. It began during the *Moscow* rescue. Mercy patched him up when he had a medium sized gash on his forearm. But they're too shy to do anything about it, so Hal discreetly asked the other girls to push them together. It's as much a social venture as pleasure."

"The little old matchmaker at work," grinned Erica. She could picture the twosome together. Johnson: tall, thin, young, with a boyish face and freckles, hair red enough to be mistaken for an Ioan instead of the Mimnite he was. *Polaris* was his first assignment since graduating from the academy.

Mercy Thompson of Earth was the young woman in question. Small, barely one hundred fifty three centimeters tall, with shoulder-length auburn hair and a happy disposition, she too was on her first mission in the Space Service. She was twenty, perhaps twenty-one, Erica remembered. Medical Technicians went through the academy quicker than others.

"Everyone has been reminded about the time of the ceremony?" asked Traynor on a serious note. "Also, did you stress the time differential? I made remarks to it in my other speeches, but did I remind them of Larandra's thirty-hour day during the last talk?" Nater nodded affirmative.

"You reminded them. Anyway, each crew member was given a sheet explaining the time differential, and covering the procedure of the ceremony," the security man assured Traynor.

"Including dress whites?"

"Including dress whites."

"May we join you, Captain?" a voice asked from

behind Nater. The huge Ganymedan stepped aside to reveal Maria McMasters and Robert Goldman. Goldman had spoken.

"Certainly. Come in." Traynor welcomed.

"Are you planning to go out soon, sir?" McMasters asked.

"I assume we'll be going out at any time," Erica quickly answered for the Captain. "If we can drag these two away from discussing business. Why don't you come along?"

"Thank you," Maria replied.

"Come on, Maria, smile. We're on shore leave!" Traynor said.

"I'm sorry, sir," replied the girl. "But I have a feeling something is going to happen; something bad."

"Oh come on," Nater laughed. "What could happen on such a joyous occasion?"

Elsewhere on Larandra, in the office of the Speaker of the People's House, Dratvin Pasteur was angrily speaking with two assistants.

"Traynor, of all men!" raved the Speaker. "This could upset our plans totally!"

"I don't understand, sir," one of the two spoke up.

"Word of my disagreement with Traynor has, I'm sure, been recorded in the service's master computers," explained Pasteur. He crossed the room and sat behind his desk, his eyes angry slits as he spoke. "It's enough that I'm going to be the center of attention after the 'accident' tomorrow. There's going to be an investigation. But our disagreement, trivial though it may seem to some people, being on file, will cause the Space Service to conduct it's own investigation, and not suffice with the local report.

"I can handle a police investigation, but the Space Service is a different thing."

"Sir, what if we dispose of the service people now, before the ceremony? We have agents following them," the second man suggested.

Pasteur paused, considering the merit of the suggestion.

"A good idea," answered the Speaker, after a moment. "Have it done."

The foursome stepped confidently along the busy sidewalk. The sidewalk was crowded with scores of people, both natives of the city and outsiders, coming from all parts of the planet, and a number of offworlders also participating in the celebration. A number of streets in the central part of Collova had been closed to all but emergency traffic, to allow the huge masses of people freer movement, not having to worry about being crowded tightly onto the sidewalk.

It was along one of the blocked streets the four *Polaris* crew members were travelling. They were attracting stares from the people they passed, not only for their uniformed appearance, but for the fact that a great number of Larandrans had never encountered Pronethans before.

"Walking with ye does have its advantages, Vlres," laughed Shawn O'Leery. "The people believe ye to be a monster and are quick to duck out of the way." Myra Shanesey, on his right, slapped him across the shoulder.

"Be on your best today, Shawn O'Leery," she reprimanded him. "None of your incessant arguing with Vlres."

"Do not worry, Myra Shanesey," Major Kran spoke up. "There will be no quarreling today."

O'Leery laughed, stopping to gaze in the huge display window of a shop.

"Interesting," he said, gazing into the glass.

"What is so interesting?" asked Myra. She glanced

into the shop, which proved to be a bakery. "Surely ye can't be hungry yet?!"

"I am always hungry," O'Leery replied in a loud voice. In much quieter tones he continued, "Two men are watching us."

"Everybody's watching us," she laughed.

"True, but everybody except those two continue on their way after a moment."

"Maybe they're looking for a certain store," speculated the girl, uneasily. She didn't want to believe there were men watching them, but the sure tones of her companion worried her.

"What are you two discussing?" Vlres interrupted.

Quickly they explained O'Leery's fears. Kran joined the group from where she had been standing, listening to the crowd. She was also filled in.

"I thought there must be an explanation for the uncomfortable feeling I had been experiencing," the Major remarked. "I sensed presences interested in us."

"Perhaps we should inform the Captain," suggested Myra Shanesey.

"And if they're tagging along for our protection?" countered O'Leery. "Wouldn't we look foolish."

"I agree," added Kran. "Even more so after the anti-Republic speech given by the man Pasteur. We could cause an extremely embarrassing incident."

O'Leery again glanced into the window, scrutinizing the men in question in the reflection off the glass. One was tall, powerfully muscled, with a nose pushed to one side of his face. The man did not leave the Ioan with a pleasant impression.

His companion was considerably shorter, overweight, and balding. O'Leery judged the shorter man to be serveral years older than his tall companion.

"We shall keep a watchful eye on them," Kran decided.

In another part of the city, four young officers from the *Polaris* entered a small cantina they had come upon. Clancy O'Hanrahan and Rene Millerand were engaged in a heated discussion of the merits of the governments of their respective worlds, which were both monarchies.

"What'll you gentlemen have?" a waiter asked after they had been seated.

O'Hanrahan and Millerand were too involved with their discussion to answer. Fred Peterson listened intently, enraptured with the talk of a governmental system so different from his home, Lunar, which was a democracy. Only David Lornton heard the waiter's question. He ordered drinks for the group. When the drinks came, the Vendran claimed his and settled back to enjoy the atmosphere, and the argument.

It was common for O'Hanrahan and Millerand to argue as they were doing. Their home worlds were both possessed of glorious self-images. Europa's main contribution to the Republic was the Royal Medical Academy. So superior were the RMA's training facilities that students flocked from the other worlds of the Republic to apply for admittance. Badrak-Badral, the twin-city capital of Europa, was constantly crowded with visiting dignitaries, and assorted others, pleading their case for a particular applicant's admittance to the academy. Other than the RMA, Europa, one of Jupiter's moons, was for the most part self-sufficient, with its huge, domed enclosures and underground installations.

Io, O'Hanrahan's home, was also a monarchy, ruled by members of the earliest families to erect the domed enclosures on Io. Ioans were possessed of the inherent pride that was common in their Scotch-Irish forefathers. Consequently, Ioans were quick and eager to talk about their home world. Their reknown had spread through the empire in two areas. As engineers, loans were hard pressed to find equals, and it was seldom, if ever, that an equal was found in the area of neutronium-drive engines.

Io's second claim to fame lay in the fine brand of whiskey it exported—said to be the best-tasting alcoholic beverage in the Republic.

"Ha! King Louis makes your Edward look like a backwater bumpkin by comparison!" laughed Millerand.

Lornton tuned out the two, settling back to enjoy his drink. He sipped the orange-colored liquid, the finest Drinan brandy available, and observed the people entering and leaving the cantina. David Lornton was a people watcher, from principle and habit. On his home planet, it was a matter of life and death to be ever alert. One slip could be fatal. The heavy-gravity Vendrans constantly experienced required its inhabitants' respect.

Lornton himself was a relative newcomer to the Space Service. He had never been outside his home star system, having attended the academy branch on Mimnon. Seldom even, had he visited the other worlds of his star system. When he received the chance, Lornton availed himself of the opportunity to study different people and cultures. With an eye on an eventual command in the Space Service, the young weapons specialist realized the need for experiences such as this one on Larandra.

Because of his continuing watchfulness, Lornton noticed the newcomers to the cantina as they entered. Six men together call attention, but the other *Polaris* crewmen were totally involved in their discussion. Each was describing to his companions, in great detail, his home world.

The new patrons seated themselves at a small table against one wall. Lornton observed them as inconspicuously as possible, noting fleeting glances in the servicemen's direction. The mysterious men would whisper among themselves after each glance.

Much of the population of the colonial planets held the Space Service in great awe, and the young weapons officer had almost convinced himself the group of Larandrans were just curious about the servicemen, when an event occurred that caused him to revise his opinion. One, a huge specimen of a man with broad shoulders and bushy black eyebrows, reached into a pocket and removed a small object, into which he spoke. Lornton realized then that group of patrons must have the *Polaris* crewmen under surveillance. Apparently Bushy Eyebrows was the leader, and he was receiving instructions from his commander.

The man was listening intently to the small machine he was trying unsuccessfully to conceal. Several times he nodded at the machine. The others of his little group had pulled their chairs closer to the large man and were straining to catch a word of the conversation.

Apparently satisfied, Bushy Eyebrows returned the machine to his pocket. Lornton continued glancing sideways at the man, carefully watching his every move. The man glanced casually over at the *Polaris* men, and Lornton, the ever-alert people watcher, noticed the change in the man's facial expression. It seemed to the Vendran that this man was having great difficulty trying not to smile. Casually the large Larandran whispered to his companions. They each made rapid movements under their tunics.

Several things happened at once.

David Lornton, reacting with the speed only a Vendran could possess, became a flurry of motion. One stout Vendran leg, propped against the table support, extended in an explosion of power, pushing the table into the other *Polaris* men, knocking them off their seats.

Powering off his other leg, firmly planted on the

floor. Lornton shot himself into the air, somersaulting some two meters above the floor, to land on a table top over four meters from his takeoff spot. Legs coiled like giant springs, Lornton lept off the table in a dive to the floor.

Clancy O'Hanrahan started to voice his displeasure at being thrown to the floor so violently. The hum of hand lasers firing through the point where he had been sitting quickly quieted him.

Patrons screamed and dove to the floor. One luckless customer had no chance to react, or even scream, as an errant beam burned a fist-sized hole in his chest. His eyes widened in disbelief as he stared at the damage the laser had done. Slowly he sank to the floor, quite dead.

The assassins were standing, searching for their victims in the crowd of people crawling along the floor. These men were confident of their superior position, having been told the men they were after would not be carrying weapons. They were not prepared for a counterattack.

The chairs of the cantina were made of a strong hardwood, similar to though much tougher than oak. The wood was from a tree native to Larandra, and the owners of the cantina had selected that particular wood because of the seeming inability of the natives to destroy the wood without resorting to the use of tools. Yet, Lornton hardly strained as he snapped the legs off two chairs beside him.

The young weapons specialist rose and flung one of the chair legs, and was back on the floor before the assassins could bring their weapons to bear on the Vendran. Thrown by any man, a block of wood the size of the chair leg could be a dangerous instrument. Backed by the muscles of a Vendran, the object was deadly. It struck the nearest gunman, a short, weasel-faced fellow, full in the face, caving in his skull and killing him instantly.

His companions, seeing his sudden collapse, stopped their hunt in surprise. Lornton took advantage of the inaction of the Larandrans. He quickly flung four more of the deadly missiles and dropped flat again. He was rewarded with four different screams, telling him each had struck its mark.

The last man, the leader, realizing he no longer held the upper hand, fired several random laser blasts and dove through the large window of the cantina, landing in the street amidst a shower of plastiglass. Quickly, Bushy Eyebrows rose to his feet and ran off.

Rene Millerand was the first to attempt rising from the floor. When there was no sound of lasers filling the air, he raced to the assassins, recovering one of the dropped lasers on the way. Weapon in hand, covering the five Larandrans lying still on the floor, the young Europan called for his companions' assistance. Quickly they joined him. In a moment they were armed and inspecting the Larandrans.

"Geez, David," O'Hanrahan said in awe. "Remind me not to get you mad at me. Ever!"

"That's the truth!" Peterson agreed.

"Clance, get ahold of the Captain," Lornton ordered.

The Ioan reached under his tunic and removed his personal communicator. Each of the *Polaris* personnel was carrying one. He dialed the captain's call frequency and pushed the emergency alert button. Almost immediately, Traynor's voice answered.

"Captain, this is O'Hanrahan," the youngster identified himself. "We've run into a little trouble."

"What happened? Where are you?"

"We're in a cantina in the western part of the city," began O'Hanrahan. "Some locals jumped us and we had to kill them."

"WHAT?!" came Traynor's disbelieving voice from the communicator. "Explain!"

Lornton took the communicator, identified himself, and explained the story. When he finished, the Vendran could hear his captain and several others discussing the incident. Finally Traynor came back on the line.

"I'm going to issue an 'all call'," Traynor told him. "Who's with you?"

"Besides Clance, Peterson and Millerand."

"Leave Peterson to explain to the authorities," Traynor said. "You others locate the group with Kevin Johnson and those nurses. They expected to be somewhere in that general area. Listen in to the 'all call' and you'll get their location." As an afterthought, he added, "Take those lasers. You may need them."

"Aye, sir," the Vendran answered. "Lornton out." He returned the box to O'Hanrahan, removed his own, and tuned it to the emergency frequency.

"Let's go," he ordered, a laser gripped tightly in his hand.

Kevin Johnson was feeling in high spirits as he stepped briskly along the sidewalk. Under one arm he carried several packages. On his other arm strolled Mercy Thompson, talking animatedly with the others walking abreast of the couple. In such good spirits was the young security officer that he made no complaint as his lovely companions led him into another huge clothing store.

Throughout the afternoon, the female officers had travelled from clothing store to clothing store, with brief side trips to jewelry manufacturers. In the beginning, Johnson had been bored with the entire trip. As the day progressed, though, he was able to overcome his shyness and show his interest in Mercy Thompson. As they conversed, it became apparent to each one of the reciprocal feelings of the other. By mid-afternoon, the tiny Earth girl and the redheaded security man were proudly walking hand in hand.

Having the young man along was a blessing for the women. Not only was he extremely levelheaded in the area of spending credits, but they happily discovered their escort had exceedingly good taste. They modeled different outfits for him, asking and considering his opinion of the various styles, colors, lengths, and fabrics. As a result, though each had made a number of purchases, they had not spent their credits wildly. Instead, each was deeply satisfied with her new things.

Entering the latest store, Johnson located a Z-grav chair floating in the women's section. The five women eagerly piled their packages around his chair and headed for the nearest computer terminal.

Computer terminals in clothing stores were curtained booths designed to make the customer's search through the huge store much simpler. In each booth was a computer input terminal, a visiscreen linked to the computer for display of clothing styles, and a printout terminal to provide the location of the article selected.

For proper operation of the computer installation, it was necessary for customers to enter, truthfully, the physical facts about themselves. Because often the correct information was not known, the enclosed booths provided the customer with mechanical measuring assistance. The computer required the correct height and weight of the woman, along with her physical measurements; the length of her inseam and her inner arm; the color of her hair, skin and eyes. Also, the woman told the computer what she was looking for, her favorite colors, and the styles that interested her the most.

The computer then went through its huge memory banks, correlating the information the woman had given it with the actual stock available. Once it had successfully matched clothes with person, the visiscreen lighted up and pictures of the clothes it deemed correct were presented. If the woman saw something she liked, she pushed a button marked "LOCATE," and the computer printed the location of the article on a reference sheet. Once the computer finished its run, the customer removed the reference sheet and began a manual search for the clothes. Store clerks, numerous and willing to help, aided the individuals in their search.

Liz Beaumont was the first to locate an item she felt was worth trying on. Laughing at the other girls rummaging through the racks of clothing, the auburn-haired Europan made her way to a free dressing booth. She slipped into the two-piece outfit. The knit synthetic material fit snugly in the proper places as she measured the length of the tunic top, which hung to mid-thigh. The young nurse's dignity was protected by the matching panties of the same material, which fit like a second skin.

Commander Beaumont gazed into the full-length mirror, admiring the effect of the outfit. The light blue pleased her, as it was her favorite color, and it went well with her skin coloring. The length of the tunic was as she desired, allowing a great deal of leg to be seen. Liz Beaumont was a tall girl, with long legs that she was proud of. She delighted in the comments she often received from men admirers, and was not opposed to showing her shapely limbs to attract the comments.

A familiar voice woke her from her trance.

"Hurry up, Liz," Mercy Thompson complained. "There's only one dressing booth in the area."

"I'm coming," replied the pretty nurse. She stepped out of the booth in the outfit she had tried on.

Heads turned to the statuesque young woman that wore the store's outfit as it should be worn. Men, assisting female companions in selection, voiced their admiration in the ageless method of appreciation, whistling. Mercy Thompson complimented her as Beaumont passed the youngster waiting to use the booth.

The auburn-haired beauty was smiling broadly as she appeared before Kevin Johnson, who was discussing the merits of an outfit Kathleen O'Casey had picked out and was waiting to try on. As Beaumont caught the young man's eye, he grinned and began a slow, appreciative once-over of the leggy beauty before him.

"What do you think?" she asked when he had finished the once-over. The young security officer leaned forward, his face still covered with smiles, to tell her exactly what he thought.

Fortune shone brightly on Lieutenant Kevin Johnson at that moment, for in leaning forward, he narrowly avoided a laser blast aimed for him. Instead, the blast struck the stuffed Z-grav chair he was seated in, producing a hole from front to back.

Johnson's reflexes, drilled into him day after day at the Space Service Academy, were lightning-quick. One arm reached out and gripped O'Casey's wrist, dragging her to the floor in his dive. As he hit the floor, his free arm shot forward and yanked the legs out from under Beaumont, rooted to her spot in terror. The girl flopped to the floor hard. Several lasers cut through the air where she had been standing.

Johnson pushed and dragged the women to some safety behind a huge pillar. Taking a quick look around, he saw that Beth Maxwell and Dawn Feather had taken refuge behind another pillar. That left only Mercy to account for.

The young woman in question, not realizing the dangerous situation on the store's floor, stepped casually from the dressing booth. In horror, Johnson watched as the five assassins turned their weapons on the unsuspecting girl.

"DOWN!" he yelled at the top of his lungs. The girl, not understanding, took another step and half turned, attempting to locate the origin of the order. Fortune, which had shone so brightly for Kevin Johnson, returned to aid the young Earth girl. Her movement had been enough to throw off the aim of the gunmen so only two lasers struck her. One flashed across her arm, while the second created a pencil-thin hole through her left thigh. Crying in pain, the girl collapsed to the floor.

Anger, blood rage, welling up inside the young Mimnite, caused him to lose his head for a second. Only a firm hand in his kept Johnson from rashly charging the five men. As his head cleared, he thankfully squeezed the hand that had held him. Commander O'Casey smiled in return.

Johnson carefully reviewed the situation. Five men with lasers. Apparently the store security had been taken care of. Over a hundred innocent bystanders in the immediate area. Himself and five women from *Polaris* as the targets. The five men were attempting to surround the six service officers.

A workman's kit lay nearby, dropped by a technician when the fighting started. Johnson jumped out, grabbed it, and leaped back. Lasers criss-crossed the point he'd jumped to.

Safely behind the pillar, he opened the kit and dumped the contents before him. Most of the tools were ordinary and useless. There was a laser probe in the kit, though, and Johnson smiled. The probe was similar to the Space Service tool used by computer technicians. This probe was evidently used in the repair of the fitting terminals. Once, in an advanced weaponry class at the academy, Johnson's instructor had been lecturing on makeshift weapons, and had demonstrated the ease in which a laser probe could be turned into a weapon.

Carefully the youngster broke the glass outer casing as he remembered his instructor had done. He then opened the inner casing of the tubular tool and scraped a small contact with his fingernail, eliminating the override fail-safe connection. He rose and carefully aimed, sighting squarely into the chest of one of the gunmen, who had separated from the others and had just achieved position to fire on the *Polaris* personnel.

There was a bright flash in his hands as he touched the "on" button. When he opened his eyes, Johnson could see that his aim had been true, striking his target squarely in the chest. Seeing the others paused in surprise, Johnson used the break to sprint the ten meters separating himself and the dead man, diving behind the body as the men recovered from their shock and fired at him. One beam struck a leg, burning a gash in the calf muscle. Stifling a scream of pain, Johnson groped and finally came up with his victim's laser pistol.

Beth Maxwell answered the communicator's beep instantly. Interrupting the captain's "all call," she filled him in on the situation. She gave her location in response to a quick interrupting question from David Lornton. Lornton then informed both Traynor and Maxwell that the computerized interlock locator on his comunicator placed him two blocks from Maxwell's position. Traynor asked if Johnson was returning fire. The blonde nurse replied negatively, but quickly cancelled her response when Johnson bobbed up and fired the captured laser at the would-be killers.

Johnson fired and a second attacker went down. The three remaining Larandrans ducked to safety, realizing their unarmed victims were now armed and fighting back. Both sides ceased firing, maneuvering for position. The Larandrans, though realizing they were in a fight, still were confident they would complete their mission. The assassins had no way of knowing that the agents detailed to do away with David Lornton's group had failed miserably. Nor could they know that three *Polaris* crewmen were angrily making their way to the store where their companions were being attacked.

The huge entrance doors burst open and the compact figure of David Lornton bounced through. Against the pull of approximately one Earth gravity, his Vendran muscles, used to a gravitational pull of over two and a half Earth Gs, sent the squat weapons officer in leaps of better than six meters, easily clearing the tall racks of clothing at the same time.

On each bounce Lornton oriented himself to the action across the store. He identified his own people on the first bounce, while locating the enemy on the second. He had covered over half the width of the store before the Larandran agents realized his presence. They spun around and began firing at him as he rose into the air each time. His return fire sent them ducking for cover again.

Millerand and O'Hanrahan burst through the entrance doors as Lornton landed from a long bounce and stayed on the floor. The security men from *Polaris* split, Millerand moving left while O'Hanrahan went right. Each moved carefully, orienting themselves to the store. Stepping around racks of clothes, they avoided the many crawling people attempting to escape the store without injury.

After several minutes of careful maneuvering, Millerand and O'Hanrahan had successfuly located and flanked the three gunmen. Lornton spotted his partners and gave the signal to fire. The three-pronged attack became four when Kevin Johnson, realizing friendlies had joined him, added his laser to the fight.

One man rose to return fire. A laser beam passed

through his head, killing him instantly. Another man had not sought cover from a four sided attack. With his two companions dead, the third man jumped up, firing his laser, and attempted to flee. Four lasers hit him and he collapsed, dead.

The three newcomers joined Johnson as he tried to stand.

"Everything OK?" Lornton asked anxiously.

"Don't know," Johnson winced. "I've got a burn in the calf. It's deep, but should be all right. Mercy caught two blasts! Arm and leg! Don't know how bad." Johnson, leaning on Millerand's shoulder, hobbled toward the injured girl, being treated by the *Polaris* nurses.

"Any others hurt?" Millerand asked.

"No," Johnson replied. "Better get hold of the Captain." Directing his interests to the nurses surrounding the injured girl, he stood by as they attended the limp body. "How is she?"

"Fortunate," replied Liz Beaumont, now fully recovered from her attack of fright and once more the efficient nurse. "The burns aren't too serious. They look worse than they are. Quite a cute hole drilled through her leg, but nothing important-was hit, just flesh and muscle. Lucky for her! The arm is just burnt." She noticed the seared trouser leg and wicked burn in Johnson's calf. She jumped over to the young man. "Set him down, Rennie." She commanded. She set about examining the burn, and pronounced it ugly but not terribly serious. She bound it with a piece of cloth from his already torn pants leg.

"Captain says he commandeered a jet car and should be here soon," O'Hanrahan told the group. "Also, Dickson and Makem didn't respond to the 'all call.' "

"Don't know where they could be?" mused Lornton. "Anybody seen them?" he asked the *Polaris* personnel assembled. All shook their heads.

Collova city police arrived first, in force. Heavy laser pistols in hand, they surrounded the non-Larandrans. The security men from *Polaris* attempted to explain the incident as the police made ready to arrest the visitors. Witnesses interrupted the police to corroborate the story. Still, the police prepared to take the men and women of the Space Service to the police station.

An imposing blond figure, easily forty centimeters taller than the crowd of Larandrans, pushed his way toward the messy women's section. The people from *Polaris* instantly recognized the giant as a Ganymedan and a friend. They also knew that with Hal Nater would be their Captain.

Nater was allowed to pass, and in a moment had arrived at the police perimeter. Traynor followed in the wake of his tall aide and began conversing with a police officer. The Captain's remarks received instant action from the police officer. The man stepped out of the way, allowing Traynor and Nater to enter the ring. The officer also passed other *Polaris* crew members to a total of ten. He quickly sealed the break in the ring before the mass of people interested in the activity could break through. Traynor was immediately directed to the officer in charge.

"What's happening? What's going on here?" Traynor demanded of the officer.

"Excuse me, sir," the man answered. "But who are you?"

"Traynor, Captain USR *Polaris*," was the quick reply. "These are my people you're attempting to arrest."

"You're their commander?"

"That's right. And who are you?"

"Lieutenant Atvar of the Collova Police Force," the man replied pleasantly. "We aren't arresting them. Just taking them in for questioning."

Hildy Bennett noticed the small knot of people kneeling farther back. It appeared to her someone had been injured. She tugged at Nater and the two headed back toward the group. An officer made an attempt to stop the couple, but Nater, a man demanding respect with or without a laser, made it apparent to the young man that they were passing. The Ganymedan nurse was aghast when she recognized the two victims.

"How're they doing?" Bennett demanded of Liz Beaumont.

"Major, am I glad to see you," Beaumont sighed, relieved. "They'll be OK, I'm pretty sure. You might check 'em over though. We dressed them as best we could. Do you have any dianzamene capsules? Mercy's not hurt bad, but she's in a bit of pain." Bennett reached under her tunic to the belt of her skirt and removed a pouch. She extracted two capsules of the synthetic wonder drug, dianzamene. Dianzamene was non-addictive, good for any pain from the smallest headache to the most serious of battle injuries. She gave one to Mercy Thompson, who had regained consciousness, and offered the other to Kevin Johnson.

"No thank you, ma'am," Johnson declined. "They made us operate with worse from the pain simulator at the academy. And I don't like drugs."

"It's your leg," she replied, smiling.

"How's Mercy?" Johnson asked. "Not bad?"

"Just fine," replied Bennett.

"They told me, but I wanted to make sure," he continued.

"Hear that, Mercy?" Bennett turned and winked at the girl. "Looks like young Mr. Johnson has quite an interest in you." Johnson's face became as red as his hair, to the amusement of the *Polaris*'s nurses.

Captain Traynor stepped into the field of vision of the two young people on the floor.

"Major Bennett, how are they?"

"Fine, Captain," she answered.

"Mercy, how're you feeling?" Traynor asked softly, kneeling beside the injured girl.

The Captain's attention caught the young woman unprepared. After several moments of confusion, she stuttered out an answer.

"F-fine sir. Thanks to Kevin."

Traynor smiled at her. "Very capable young man, wouldn't you say?"

"Yes, sir. I would." She smiled.

A stir in the crowd caused Traynor to rise. The crowd parted and six people stepped through. Traynor recognized five of the newcomers as *Polaris* personnel. Kran and Shanesey led the way, with Vlres, O'Leery and Peterson bringing up the rear. The only unfamiliar person, a short, balding, overweight man, marched between them. The three *Polaris* crewmen in the rear had laser pistols, drawn and pointed at the fourth man.

"Good day, Captain," Major Kran said. "You are safe."

"Yes," replied Traynor. "Who's the fellow with you?"

"This here fella and a friend, tried to do us in," Shawn O'Leery laughed. "His friend tried a mite too hard."

"This is one of them?" Traynor asked.

"Affirmative," Vlres responded.

"Well now," Traynor said. "I think we'll find out what this is all about." Twenty angry Space Service members crowded toward the Larandran assassin.

The city of Collova was decked out in its finest.

The ceremonies of independence, held at the fairgrounds, attracted the majority of the population of the city, along with a great number of people from other parts of Larandra. The people filling every inch of space at the fairgrounds were dressed in their best clothes for the celebration.

A huge platform, even larger than the one at the space port, had been erected for the ceremony. Several hundred seats had been arranged on the platform, for the representatives of the USR, the members of both houses of Larandra's legislature, the many high-ranking officials invited to the ceremony, and of course, the Premier, Vice-Premier, and speaker of the People's House. Traynor was seated in a chair alongside the three most important members of the Larandran government.

Eight seats were empty in the *Polaris* personnel section. The seats designated for Reg Dickson, Millie Makem, Kevin Johnson, and Mercy Thompson, along with Peterson, Millerand, O'Hanrahan, and Trout were noticeably vacant. The remaining crew members wore their dress whites.

Dratvin Pasteur was the first to step to the microphone to address the people of Larandra and, through the radio links, the governmental bodies of the member worlds of the United Space Republic.

"Friends, countrymen, people of Larandra. Today is the culmination of our struggle to throw off the yoke of colonialism! No longer are we at the mercy of the Interplanetary Council!" His words brought instant crowd approval.

"It has been a difficult fight, my friends," Pasteur continued. "An uphill struggle against many obstacles. There are forces working against the advancement of the colonial planets into self-sufficient governments. These forces believed they had control of the Interplanetary Council. The vote on Larandra's independence has shown them the error of their thinking. Do not believe for one minute, however, that this power has given up the fight."

Pasteur continued for over twenty minutes, blasting the Council and the power behind the Council. Never once did he identify this elusive power specifically, but through his implications, everyone was well aware that he was speaking of Earth. The crowd absorbed his every word, cheering wildly.

"And now, my friends," he ended his speech. "I must go. I would like to stay for the entire ceremony, but the duties of my office are never-ending." He picked up his papers and started for one of the ramps off the platform.

The master of ceremonies thanked him and introduced the representative from the United Space Republic, Alexander Traynor of the *Polaris*. Traynor reached the microphone as Pasteur reached the top of the stairs. Miraculously, one of the missing security men appeared at the bottom of the steps and started up.

"Don't go away yet, Mr. Speaker," Traynor said into the microphone. "The festivities are just getting started." Pasteur started for another exit, but a *Polaris* man appeared there also. A glance told the Larandran that all his exits were cut off by Traynor's men.

"Friends, greetings. Congratulations, Larandrans!" The crowd noise forced Traynor to pause. When the people became quieter, he continued. "Friends, I had a speech planned for you today, but events of the past thirty hours have made me reconsider.

"Yesterday, while exploring this fabulous city of Collova, my crew and myself came under attack by then unknown assassins. Several of my crew were injured, including two critical cases and two others not seriously injured; all were transported to *Polaris*.

"Why these assassins attacked us we had no way of

knowing. Only through the brave and commendable actions of my crew are we still here."

Pasteur made an attempt to jump off the platform. Hal Nater, Shawn O'Leery, and David Lornton prevented him from leaving, and escorted him to the microphone. Several members of the crowd made motions to come on the platform and defend Pasteur, but the awesome figure of Hal Nater, laser pistol in hand, quickly showed them the error of their thinking. The Larandrans settled down.

Pasteur was frantic. He checked his watch, shrieked when he saw the time, and struggled to get free. When his struggles did not cause his release, Pasteur began screaming.

"You don't understand! I've got to get away! We've got to get away! Please, let me go! I've got to get away from this platform!"

"Commander Shawn O'Leery was fortunate enough to capture one of the assassins. We questioned him at length."

"Traynor, we've got to get away! There's a bomb on the platform!" Pasteur's voice carried into the microphone and was broadcast to the audience. People jammed against the platform began screaming and pushing themselves away.

"There is no bomb! Listen to me! There is no bomb!" Traynor's voice carried out over the crowd in a calming wave. The people in the front stopped screaming.

"As I said, there is no bomb. When the assassin was questioned, the entire plot was uncovered. The Vice-Premier was immediately informed. Before anyone arrived today, special police, with the help of a weapons expert from my crew, uncovered and disarmed the bombs planted under the platform."

The Premier had come forward from his seat and

motioned Traynor away from the microphone. Akamel Drakar accompanied the Premier.

Travlem Dean was a man of about sixty-five Earth years. His gray hair and the thick spectacles he wore belied the energy the man had for his job. Dean was truly interested in his people's welfare.

"Would you please explain what is going on, Captain Traynor?" the Premier demanded.

"Sir, there was a plot to kill everyone on this platform today," explained Traynor. "Today is probably the only time this planet will see its leaders gathered together in one place." Traynor glanced at the speaker of the People's House, now silent in the realization of the trap into which he had fallen. "All the leaders except one."

"Pasteur," Dean filled in.

"As the interim leader," continued Traynor. "He planned to set up a dictatorship on this planet. He had enough sway in the police force to have the bombing incident blamed on anyone he chose. When I arrived, it complicated things. He and I had a run-in before, and the incident is in the Space Service files. Fleet Command might hold its own investigation instead of accepting the police report as they would do with another officer."

Angela Martin carefully maneuvered herself to stand beside Traynor. She discreetly attracted his attention.

"Excuse me Mr. Premier," Traynor said. He turned to the girl. "Yes Lieutenant?"

"Major LeMay is on the communicator with *Polaris*, sir. An emergency call from Fleet Headquarters at Mimnon. We are to proceed at all speed to Mimnon base. Twelve orbital stations have been attacked. Bases twenty-one, twenty-seven, thirty-four, thirty-five, and thirty six were destroyed. Completely!"

"Make sure everyone knows what's going on. Be

ready to go in two minutes. I'll join you in a moment." She saluted him and returned to the *Polaris* people, all listening to their communicators. Traynor turned back to the Premier.

"Well sir, you heard it," Traynor smiled. "Congratulations on your independence. Wish we could stay."

"So do I, Captain," Dean replied, extending his hand. Traynor shook it. The Vice-Premier also shook Traynor's hand.

"Mr. Vice-Premier, it was good seeing you," said Traynor. "Hope I'll be seeing you again." He started toward his people. The three *Polaris* men turned their prisoner over to the local police and joined their captain. As if struck by a sudden thought, Traynor stopped and turned back to the Premier.

"Sir, about our things at the hotel. Would you please hold them for us? We'll come back for them as soon as possible."

The Premier nodded his agreement and Traynor hurried to his crew.

VI

"Shall we get this thing started?" Alexander Traynor spoke up as the last officer entered. "I assume you all know our orders. Proceed to Mimnon for recovery work at one of the destroyed orbital stations to be assigned to us then. We are executing those orders at all possible speeds."

"Captain, why have you ordered a course change?" Victoria Spencer asked.

"Captain, not to proceed directly to Mimnon is to disregard orders, and is an offense that can result in your being removed as commander of *Polaris*. To disregard a direct order would be considered mutiny." Traynor turned to the speaker, Carl Nelson. The executive officer read something in the captain's face, telling him that the captain was not to be tested at this moment. Nelson settled back in his chair, avoiding Traynor's eyes.

"For those of you who are worried," Traynor began, giving Nelson a meaningful glance. "The exact wording of the message does not specify the route we are to take. Therefore, I am taking the route I believe will be the most effective.

"The 'why' of our course change can best be answered by Major Marshall."

The tall Triton stood and moved around the table until he was standing beside the mini-tank. The captain settled down in his seat. He knew what to expect from

Marshall's talk.

"When examining the data sent by Command on the enemy attacks on the orbital stations, it occurred to me to take a planetary placement reference. What showed up was an odd coincidence, which I would like to present to you."

The dark-haired scientist reached down and snapped on the mini-tank. The small navigational device, a scaled-down version of the huge model on the bridge, was programmed for a Barnard system projection. The star was the central figure of the projection, which was large enough for the entire group assembled, ten in all, to have a clear view. Each of the fourteen planets, proportionally scaled, was present in the picture. A small light between the nineth and tenth planetary ring represented *Polaris*.

"What you are seeing is the Barnard system as it would appear at this moment in time," Marshall explained. "If I have correctly programmed the computer, when I touch the project button again, what we shall see will be the Barnard system as it was when the simultaneous attack on the twelve orbital stations took place." He touched the button and the projection shifted.

"Excellent," Marshall smiled. The officers gazed intently at the tank, trying to grasp the coincidence Marshall was speaking of. "The enigma becomes clearer. Let me add one more thing." He touched another control. "I have just added the orbital stations that were attacked." Lights appeared near the planets in question. "The pattern should be evident."

Puzzled faces stared back at him. No one saw any pattern. Traynor did not bother answering, for he knew what to look for.

"Surely you must see the pattern," Marshall asked, surprised. "You, of course, see it Colonel N'goto." The black shook his head. "Colonel Nelson? Miss Spencer, surely as a navigator you must have detected the pattern." The two answered negatively.

Marc De Gaulle stared at the rows of lights. He couldn't imagine what kind of pattern the scientist was talking about. Eight planets extending out from the sun. Twelve orbital stations.

It was as if someone hit him over the head. His eyes widened! He checked himself, calming the inner excitement. Carefully, like the trained doctor he was, De Gaulle rechecked his facts. The eight planets were located, at that precise moment, on the same side of the sun. It was almost a straight line from the center of the solar system to Xi Barnard, the tiny airless planet that was fourteenth from the sun. He was almost ready to explode with his answer when his sharp eyes noticed an even odder coincidence of the planets in question. From the angle of the tank he was viewing, it appeared all the orbital stations were on the same side of their respective planets.

"The planets are in alignment!" He exploded. "And the stations are on the same side! Must happen once in a blue moon!"

"A quaint way of putting it, Doctor," Marshall smiled. "But you are quite correct. There was planetary and orbital station alignment. An excellent time to mount a multi-pronged simultaneous attack if attacking from out of the star system in this direction." His finger traced a line away from the crippled stations perpendicular to the imaginary line that would be the planetary alignment.

"If they were attacking from that side, why didn't they attack Station Eighteen?" Ben Peters asked.

"The data sent to us lists the battleship *Bosworth* and the cruiser *Nottingham* in synchronized orbit with station eighteen around Vendra. Apparently, the threat of the added firepower of the ships was enough to keep them from attacking."

"An interesting theory," Nelson said icily. "But what is the point?"

"The point, Colonel, is that we are headed in the general direction of those crippled stations that are left. We might be able to pick up a trace of the enemy craft and discover some information about the location of their home." Traynor replied in like tones.

"Instead of taking a direct course to Mimnon, which is heading three-forty by twenty, we are taking a more circuitous route. Heading forty-five by three-fifty. We'll make a large arc around the sun and head to Mimnon."

"Captain, in my opinion, to do as you are intending is to disregard and disobey a direct order," Carl Nelson snapped.

"Disregard?" Traynor contemplated the thought for a moment. "No, I don't think I'm disregarding the order. We are proceeding to Mimnon. As for disobeying my superior, while I may not be complying with the intent of the order, I have not disobeyed the order as it was worded. We are travelling at emergency speed at this moment."

"Sir, if you persist in this action, I will be forced to call for implementation of Fleet Regulation Book Four, Section Seven, Paragraph One," Nelson said.

"*Polaris* will carry out my orders, " Traynor replied slowly and deliberately, spacing each word with great care. "Take your vote."

Nelson turned to the others present. Under Fleet regulations, a panel of senior officers could vote the Captain unfit to command. To relieve the Captain, the panel's vote had to be unanimous.

Point 'E' of Regulation 471 was specific as to which officers were to make up the panel that voted on the Captain's fitness aboard a Fleet heavy cruiser.

"I vote removal," Nelson said. He turned to the Captain and smiled, then sat.

"Removal," N'goto seconded.

"Removal," Corensky laughed.

"Remain," Kran spoke up in a monotone.

"You can't be serious!" Nelson yelled, exploding from his chair. "He's disobeying a direct order! The regulations require an incompetent captain to be removed from duty!"

"That they do," Kran replied flatly. "If Captain Traynor were incompetent, I would vote so. However, I know that he is not."

"You know, do you?" Nelson said sarcastically. "Well, Major, when we're all dying, remember that you're the one who let this fool kill us!" Nelson sat back down. All faces turned to the captain to see his reaction to Nelson's charges.

There was no expression on his face. His jaw was set determinedly. Perhaps, Erica LeMay thought, she caught a flicker in his eyes. Anger, and something else. Hurt. . .betrayal? It was there only for an instant, then carefully masked, even to her.

"Perhaps you'd like to hear my vote?" Marc De Gaulle asked humorously. "I'm thirty-two years old. I've been a doctor for several years. In my time, I have known only three men who truly cared for the people they were responsible for. One is my king, Louis XII. His son, Phillip Louis. And Alexander Traynor. To believe that he is incompetent is to believe that my king is incompetent. Captain Traynor would never put his crew in danger unless he thought it was necessary for the wellbeing of the entire Republic."

"If you believe that, you are as big a fool as he is, Europan," Nelson interrupted disgustedly.

"Can't you ever shut up?" Erica LeMay demanded. "We listened to you rant on. Have the decency to let the doctor finish. Or is that too much to ask of you?"

Carl Nelson froze. Slowly he turned to focus on the blonde engineer, who defiantly returned his stare. Nelson's face bore a look of anger and hate, and it was directed at the assistant chief engineer.

LeMay held her eyes locked into his. Everything seemed distant and unreal as she held his eyes; those dark and cruel eyes; locked in what was the most crucial test of her self-confidence. No one could help her now.

The moments seemed like hours. Once she felt she had to give up, but a wave of determination reinforced her. She held out until, after what seemed like an eternity, Nelson dropped his eyes to the table. A small smile of triumph tugged at the corners of the Europan girl's mouth.

". . .and therefore, I vote remain," De Gaulle finished with a flourish.

"I believe your four-seven-one has failed," Traynor said, savoring each word. "Now, if we can get back to business, this briefing is dismissed." The assembled group stood and saluted. The five Earth officers marched stiffly out. The others crowded around Traynor.

"Whew!" sighed the Captain. "That's as close to a four-seven-one as I ever want to be! Thanks Kran, Marc."

"Captain, if you were truly incompetent, I would have voted as they did," the Pronethan informed him. "But, as I informed the Colonel, I know."

"Well, I know what I know," Marc De Gaulle laughed.

"A truly intelligent statement, doctor," Marshall commented. "I must say, you do have a remarkable way of putting things."

"Alex knows what I mean."

Traynor grinned. "Yes, I do, Marc. And thank you."

"And me?" asked Erica LeMay.

"And you," Traynor answered. "But we have work to do." He turned his gaze on Theodore Marshall. "I do hope your theory has some merit." The man nodded in agreement.

Outside the briefing room an angry Carl Nelson stormed down the corridor. The senior officers of *Polaris* kept in step with him.

"What do we do now?" Ben Peters asked softly, not to disturb the exec's train of thought.

"We have to go along with him," Nelson replied angrily. He shook his head in disgust. "There's nothing we can do now, short of actually taking over the ship."

"That's a possibility," Corensky smiled savagely. "We could teach a few of these outworlders a lesson."

Nelson stopped short, and to the astonishment of the others, he seemed to be smiling.

"Obviously Majors Kran and De Gaulle are too close to the Captain to make their decision on the four-seven-one with total objectivity. Therefore, substitutes should vote in their place." He turned his smiling face on Victoria Spencer and Ben Peters. "What better substitutes than the chief navigator and chief pilot?" His smile became infectious as his companions began to understand his plan.

"Erica," Traynor pulled the girl aside as the remaining officers hurried out of the briefing. "Get a couple of good engineers and meet me in my quarters in about fifteen minutes. I have something I think you'd like to see. I've been keeping it under wraps because of orders from the top, but I think we may need it soon."

"What is it, Alex?" the girl asked.

"I'll tell you then," he answered and walked on. She called her acknowledgement, and headed the other direction down the corridor.

The four examined the diagrams layed out on the table. Alex Traynor explained the papers as best he could, but it was evident the others understood the diagrams without his aid. He contented himself with briefly explaining the background of the papers.

"As I said, my chief engineer on *Geronimo* worked out the theoretical principle. He adapted our engines and we increased our speed capability between fifty and seventy-five percent. That's twenty-five percent faster than the enemy's projected capability."

"Where did you get these, Captain?" Shawn O'Leery asked.

"They're copies of the original diagrams drawn by Anlat Tramar, my chief engineer on *Geronimo*," replied Traynor, sitting down. He had a working knowledge of the neutronium-drive engines, but he was in the company of experts, and chose the better part of valor. "I've been told to keep it to myself while Fleet specialists test it, but I think they'll let this one go by. Besides, no one but we four will know."

"Erica, it looks possible," Charlene McKinley spoke up. The Ioan girl was young for a commander, and Traynor was a little leery when she first showed up with the others, but Erica had picked her and he trusted the Europan's judgment.

"It'll work Char," replied LeMay, studying a page of the diagrams. "In fact, what say, Shawn, if we insulate this point by two." She stabbed at a spot on the diagram. "Then attach a double power relay here and here," pointing at another diagram page. "And fit a 648 transcormatic plate at point K, instead of a 254 plate." O'Leery grinned at her. McKinley nodded, understanding. Erica looked over to the captain, who wore a puzzled expression. She smiled at him.

"I think we can do better than this," was all she said.

"How long?" asked Traynor.

"In sub-light, two days."

"Can't drop out of neutronium drive," Traynor informed her.

"Four then. Maybe more."

"Do it."

"Captain, sensors are picking up a large number of ships at extreme range," Theodore Marshall called out, not looking up from the sensor screen at the science station. "Number of ships indeterminate. Identity of ships unknown. However, I hypothesize them to be the enemy fleet."

"Heading?"

"Ninety by twenty-five. They are reaching the outskirts of the Barnard system even now. Moving at cruise speed. Approximately one hundred seventy-five BK's." He raised up from the small screen. "They seem to be confident to the point of overconfidence."

"Wouldn't you, after destroying five orbital stations?" Traynor questioned in like tones.

"Major Kran. Contact Mimnon base. Tell them we have extreme range sensor contact with the enemy fleet, and are following them. We intend to stay at extreme range, and hopefully they'll take us home with them.

"Miss McMasters," Traynor continued, swinging his chair to face front again. "Plot a parallel course to the enemy, keeping always at extreme sensor range. Mr. Goldman, implement. You will take course corrections directly from Major Marshall."

"Sir, you can't possibly be serious!" Nelson exclaimed. He jumped up from the exec console and stepped to the command chair. "You can't do this! It's suicide!"

"Nelson, tend to your job, and I'll tend to mine. And, before you try another four-seven-one, check Regulation two-four-three, which says, in effect, that a ship's captain may countermand a direct order from his superiors in time of war, if it is in the best interest of the Republic," Traynor cooled him quickly. "In my opinion, this could be the most important mission any ship in the Fleet has ever undertaken."

"You planned to do this." Nelson told rather than asked the captain.

"If we got the chance, Colonel," grinned Traynor. "And we did. Now sit down!

"Major Kran, put me shipwide."

The Pronethan touched the correct buttons.

"Shipwide sir."

"This is the Captain," Traynor addressed the crew through the intercom in his chair arm. "Our sensors have just picked up a large fleet at extreme range, leaving the Barnard system. The identity of this fleet is unknown at this time. However, Major Marshall hypothesizes, and I agree, that this is the enemy fleet that destroyed Orbital stations twenty-one, twenty-seven, and thirty-four through thirty-six.

"A message has been sent to Fleet operations Mimnon. If we wait for a reply, though, the enemy fleet will be out of sensor range, and we may have lost our one shot at following them to their home base. Therefore, I have decided to follow the enemy fleet, dispatching marker buoys at regular intervals.

"I won't lie and say there's no danger involved in this course of action. If our sensors cannot distinguish the size of the fleet, then there is a probability that the number could total as many as twenty-five to thirty-five battleships or more, and heavy cruisers, not to mention the support ships. If even one of them discovers us, there could be serious consequences.

"Taking into consideration the danger involved, I believe the good we could do for the Republic outweighs any danger we might face. I believe this could be the most important mission a Fleet starship has ever undertaken.

"Captain out."

"Course implemented, sir," Goldman informed Traynor.

"Marshall, when you get a chance, plot. . ." Traynor began, but the lean Triton cut him off.

"Already doing it, sir," he said. "Computer is constantly revising the radio messages aboard the buoy markers."

"Excellent. Radio silence, Major Kran," said Traynor.

"Aye, sir," Kran replied.

"What have you found out, Vlad?" Carl Nelson asked the chief engineer.

"Nothing much," answered Corensky. He stood up and began pacing the room. The others remained quiet knowing this was not the time to bother the engineer. Finally, he stopped in front of Nelson's desk. "They're doing some kind of modification work on the neutronium drive. Been on it for two days now."

"What kind of work?" Francis Jenkins questioned.

"I don't know, dammit!" Corensky spun on Jenkins. "If I did, don't you think I'd tell you!"

"Stop it!" came the commanding voice of Victoria Spencer. "Fighting among ourselves won't do us any good." Jenkins nodded in resigned agreement. Corensky angrily returned to his seat. A moment of silence passed.

"I don't understand it." Nelson broke the silence. "First we follow the enemy fleet, and now he's got them working on the neutronium drive. What is he doing?"

I th-think he's g-gone nuts," Ben Peters said, in a soft voice.

"Shut up, Peters!" Corensky growled. The chief pilot winced visibly at the verbal lash to his ego.

"No, no. Don't stop, Ben." Nelson's face lit up. "Go ahead. I think you've got something."

"Well, it seems to m-me," Peters stuttered again. "That while w-we're on s-such an important mission, as h-he calls it, th-this is no t-time to be p-playing with th-the engines. I m-mean, what would h-happen if someone f-from th-that f-fleet discovered us the same time one of those people messes up the neutronium drive. W-we'd b-be s-sitting d-ducks," Peters finished shakily. The chief pilot wasn't used to the amount of attention the others were giving him.

"You know something?" Carl Nelson told the gathering. "Ben's right. Traynor is jeopardizing the safety of the whole ship. We'll have to do something about it."

"For instance?" science officer N'goto asked, his black face turned inquiringly to *Polaris*'s Executive officer.

"It appears we'll have to take the ship forcibly," Nelson said.

"Now you're talking!" Corensky laughed. Francis Jenkins mirrored the chief engineer's expression.

Victoria Spencer shook her head doubtfully. "I don't think that's wise. Won't it be classified as mutiny?"

"Victoria." Nelson spoke calmly, as if explaining something to a small child. "You know that we took the vote on the four-seven-one, with yourself and Peters as substitutes for Kran and De Gaulle. On the report we listed, as per four-seven-two, the reasons for substituting. I'm sure the review board will agree that both Kran and De Gaulle are emotionally too close to Traynor and are not able to render a logical decision."

"When you put it that way," Spencer nodded. "I suppose you're right."

"Of course I am," Nelson smiled.

"Why must we take over by force?" Spencer asked sharply.

The others smiled, all save Peters. He rarely smiled.

"Surely you don't believe the outworlders on this ship will allow a peaceful change of command." It was Francis Jenkins who spoke the common thought of the others gathered.

"If you say so," Spencer agreed, somewhat skeptically. "When do we do it?"

"You'll know!" Corensky said loudly, a wide grin spread across his ugly face.

The tall, lean Triton bent over the sensor screen of the science station. Mechanically he punched a sequence of buttons, feeding input into the computer. His eyes never left the sensor screen.

"Major Marshall, my screen reads the enemy fleet changing course again. Do you copy?" Robert Goldman addressed the science officer as he busily flipped the correct switches to allow his screen to continue monitoring the massive fleet.

"Uh, yes, Commander, I do. Forgive me. Come to course two-forty-six by thirty-five." Marshall immediately returned to the computer. So intently was he involved in the action on the visiscreen that the captain had called him twice before the dark-haired man realized someone was speaking to him.

"Mr. Marshall," Traynor said for the third time. The science officer snapped upright immediately.

"Yes, sir?"

"Any luck with the new course change?"

"No, sir."

"Keep trying."

"Aye, sir." Back to the computer. Where was the clue? It had to be there. Three and a half days, and they hadn't set course for home. What could there possibly be in the random way they were changing courses?

To puzzle Major Theodore Marshall, the bridge crew knew the problem must certainly be a difficult one. Marshall was a genius, plain and simple. His IQ ran off the scale on the service entrance exam. At the academy, he'd taught computer science classes while attending as a recruit-student.

Excluding his computer background, Marshall was a scientist of considerable reputation in more than one other field. A native of Triton, the USR's acknowledged home of science, he'd been trained in the sciences from the day he'd learned to write.

Graduating the Triton Science Academy at age nineteen, two years faster than the average Triton, Marshall attended the Service Academy.

Now thirty-five, Marshall was the top expert in computer science, and an acknowledged expert in several other scientific fields. Yet, with all his scientific expertise, Marshall could not determine any pattern to aid him in discovering the mysterious fleet's home.

There had to be a point he was missing. There was no pattern to the change in course, just like the other course changes. The nearest star that was intersected by this new course was too distant for Marshall to believe it to be the enemy fleet's home. In fact, at the speed the fleet was traveling, only two or three stars were within a reasonable time frame from their present position.

Let's see, thought Marshall, stars within a reasonable time frame. Go over that again. Last time there were five. Try seven-day time frame.

The scientist punched the proper sequence of buttons, commanding the computer to present him with the asked-for information. Slowly the computer printed the information on his screen, from most distant to nearest. Sol—six days, twenty-three hours. Barnard—three days, sixteen hours. And. . .

"Alpha Centauri!" Marshall exclaimed. Several members of the bridge crew jumped at his outburst. Traynor turned to him inquisitively.

"Yes, Mr. Marshall?"

"Sir," the man recovered his poise quickly. "After careful compilation of facts, I believe I've come across data that allows me to hypothesize the Alpha Centauri trinary as the home system of the unknown fleet.

"Impossible." The voice came from the elevator. Traynor turned to see science officer N'goto and executive officer Nelson coming onto the bridge. Apparently N'goto had heard Marshall's speech, for it was he who had spoken.

"Impossible, Colonel?" Traynor asked.

"Absolutely, sir." N'goto walked across the bridge to stand at the science station. Marshall moved out of his way. "Always has been considered so. No planets can exist orbiting a trinary. That's why Alpha Centauri was passed over in favor of Barnard's Star when space exploration first began."

"I would have to agree with Colonel N'goto, sir," Carl Nelson spoke up. He had seated himself at the exec console, but invovled himself in the conversation. "With my limited scientific background, I'd think that a planet would not be able to exist with three suns."

Traynor looked from one to the other of his senior officers.

"That's the popular theory," Traynor agreed. "But, if I remember correctly, only one scientific survey was sent to Alpha Centauri. What was it, three hundred and fifty years ago?"

"Three hundred and seventy-eight sir," Marshall interrupted him. "To be exact. Arrival, November 4, 2080, standard calendar. Survey undertaken for approximately one standard week."

"There you go," Traynor told his officers. "One week of survey. They found no planets, but they didn't venture inside of Proxima. They never investigated the big doubles."

N'goto laughed. "Closer than Proxima? A planet? Be easier to find a snowball in hell."

"Possibly," Traynor said slowly. "But let's hear the major out. Go ahead, Marshall."

"Three factors, sir. One: it's a large fleet. That would indicate a base of some kind for supply. It would not seem logical to send a fleet that large together unless they were traveling a short distance, relatively speaking.

"Two: speed. They're travelling at cruise speed; one-seventy-five BK's. A speed they would not travel unless they felt safe. Safe enough not to take evasive action to avoid leading us to their home. Also, I think we can assume they have not discovered us. Now, traveling at this speed, there are only a small number of stars the fleet could reach in a reasonable time.

"Three: the random pattern of their course changes. One might call it a textbook example of regulation maneuvers to throw off enemy tracking units. We are fortunate to have an able pilot of Mr. Goldman's caliber at the helm. Otherwise we might have been discovered by now.

"These factors indicate a star system nearby. Alpha Centauri is only four hours from us at this speed."

"An interesting hypothesis," N'goto remarked, a grin crossing his black face. "But highly implausible."

"Enemy fleet changing course, Major," Robert Goldman sung out. "Course two-ninety by twelve."

"Come to that heading, Commander." Marshall turned to the Captain. "Two-ninety by twelve passes through the Apha Centauri system."

"Coincidence," Nelson spoke up.

"They've picked up speed, sir," Goldman interrupted.

"Match them, Commander," Marshall ordered. Goldman flipped the proper switches and *Polaris* accelerated smoothly, the bridge crew hardly feeling the increased speed.

"I still say it's a coincidence," Nelson said loudly.

"We'll go on the assumption it's not," Traynor replied. "Sound red alert, Lieutenant Stuart."

"Aye, sir," the Lunarite answered. She touched the red button arranged by itself on her panel. Immediately the automated alert call sounded.

"Engineering, Corensky," came from the speaker on the arm of the command chair.

"Let me speak to Major LeMay or Commander O'Leery," Traynor spoke.

The chief engineer scowled at the intercom. "It'll take a moment, Captain." He waved a young engineering specialist over to him, and told the girl to summon LeMay. The young Lieutenant climbed the stairs to the second level and hurried to where Erica LeMay and Charlene McKinley were peering into an open access duct. The feet of another officer could be seen extending from the duct. LeMay checked a diagram she was holding.

"How's the flow rate at point L?" she asked the person in the access chute. The messenger stood patiently aside, waiting for a break before she interrupted LeMay.

"Strong as always," came the Ioan brogue of

Shawn O'Leery. "If ye'll be handin' me a flow neutralizer and a demagnetized energy-cutter, I'll be thankin' ye."

McKinley bent to hand him the tool. The messenger took this opportunity to inform Erica that the captain wanted her on the intercom. LeMay nodded and stepped over to an intercom in the wall. She thumbed the switch.

"Yes, Captain?" the young engineer asked.

"Major, how's your project coming along?'

"We can see the end now, Captain," she replied. "Commander O'Leery is installing a power relay now. After that's done, only installing a small grid plate is left."

"When do you think it'll be ready?" Traynor wanted to know.

"Let's see. The relay will take about thirty minutes more. The plate, another ninety. Add on another hour, maybe two, for testing, plus thirty minutes as a safety hedge, and there you are. Three and a half hours tops. Probably more."

"We may not have that long," was Traynor's response.

"We can only work so fast," she told him matter-of-factly.

"Do your best. Traynor out."

"LeMay out." She stepped over to the open access duct.

On the lower level, Colonel Vladimir Corensky glared evilly at the Assistant Chief engineer.

There was more than the normal number of people on the bridge as Traynor sat, his eyes fixed on the image of Proxima Centauri, still millions of kilometers away, but filling the big screen. The senior officers of each department but engineering were manning the departmental stations on the bridge. However, at each station a junior officer stood ready to assist at a moment's notice. Traynor had insisted on this procedure, over the objections of his executive officer.

"Once more!" Traynor demanded. He turned to stare at his senior science officer. The black was intimidated by Traynor's piercing blue eyes. Theodore Marshall quickly jumped in to cover N'goto's silence.

"They've vanished sir," he said. "As if they never existed."

"How could a fleet of that size simply vanish?" the captain asked loudly. N'goto still could not find a voice, so Marshall continued talking.

"The computer's working on it, sir. No theory yet. But possibly it might be linked with Proxima. After all, it was as the fleet passed it that they blinked out."

"Question, Mr. Marshall. Is it safe for us to continue following the enemy fleet?"

"I would think so," Marshall replied slowly. "It would seem difficult to believe that a race of people as intelligent as the enemy seems to be would create a device that would be dangerous to shielded starships. They, themselves are exposed to the device, whatever it is."

"I vote no," Nelson spoke up. Traynor spun the chair to face the executive officer.

"I was unaware that this ship was a democracy," Traynor said. "Follow them, Mr. Peters."

"Aye, sir," Peters answered.

Polaris moved toward the point where the enemy fleet had vanished from the sensors. As they approached within Proxima Centauri's influence, Marshall, who had stepped over to man the science station, rattled off a continuous update on the radiation level, as he monitored *Polaris*'s approach.

"Levels outside shields," Marshall informed the

crew. "Four hundred rads. Four-ten, four-twenty-five, fifty, sixty, eighty, five-hundred rads. Ship's level one hundred Rads constant. Outside levels up to five-fifty, sixty, eighty, ninety-five. Six hundred rads, Captain. Six-ten, six-twenty-five, forty, fifty." He stopped, stood and slowly turned to face Traynor.

"The radiation level sir," he said in reply to Traynor's questioning gaze. "It dropped to zero as we came out of Proxima's path."

"Strange," Traynor agreed. "But we can't worry about that. Sensor probe at full extension. I want to know everything possible about this area."

"Aye, sir," Marshall answered. Both he and N'goto bent over the science section.

Erica LeMay stood up after crawling out of the access duct. As she looked up, she came face to face with Vladimir Corensky. It startled her, but she recovered quickly.

"Colonel, this area has been restricted, by the Captain's orders. You'll have to leave."

The huge chief engineer did not answer the woman, but reached behind his back. Major LeMay was about to remind her superior again of the restriction on the area, when she saw what it was he had reached for. In his huge hand was a standard service laser, aimed at her chest. Her mouth clamped shut in stunned surprise.

Corensky grabbed the girl by the wrist and swung her behind him as the second person in the access duct crawled out. Charlene McKinley stood and stretched her cramped muscles.

"Boy, the muscles sure get tight in there, eh, Erica?" McKinley laughed. When she received no answer, she turned to locate the major. The last thing she saw, before her head exploded in pain, was a huge fist, grasping a laser pistol, and speeding toward her face. The pain was immeasurable, but, thankfully, she passed out quickly.

Shawn O'Leery heard the loud crack of fist connecting with skull, so he was somewhat prepared for the unexpected. Yet, as he came hurridly out of the duct, Corensky gripped the Ioan tightly, over his protestations, and, straining mightily, heaved the young engineer toward the railing at the edge of the upper deck. O'Leery flipped over the rail and landed heavily on his back on the lower level.

The personnel on the lower level were startled when O'Leery's body landed practically on top of them. Several rushed to him, and others immediately rushed to intercoms to notify the medical section. It was Corensky's booming voice that stopped them in their tracks.

"Get out!"

They looked up to see the chief engineer standing at the top of the stairs, a laser in one hand, Major LeMay's wrist in the other.

"Get out!" he screamed again.

They started backing out of the engineering section. Two of the young fellows made an attempt to drag O'Leery out with them.

"Leave him!" Corensky ordered. He pointed the laser at LeMay's head. "Get out!" They quickly obeyed his orders, rushing out the automatic doors. The senior officer, a commander, rushed to the nearest intercom and called the security section.

"Captain, sensors report some startling information." Marshall spoke up, performing the job N'goto should have done. "It appears there are two planets revolving around the Alpha Centauri binary. No data on planet size yet. We're too far away."

"Well, there goes that theory," Traynor smiled.

"But the most startling information is this," Marshall said. He punched a button on the console before him. Immediately the scene on the big visiscreen changed. Instead of a picture of empty deep space, the screen was filled with a picture of a rocky, barren asteriod.

"Well, what is it?" Traynor asked.

"It appears to be an artificially constructed planetoid. Notice the smooth contours, the unnatural roundness of the structure. Definitely not natural."

"Fine. What does it do?" Traynor said, impatiently.

"It appears, sir," Marshall explained, "to be a sensor-jamming device to prevent the locating of the planets within. The device is apparently in synchronized movement with Proxima Centauri.

"Also, it appears this device gives off the radiation that we ran into earlier. Possibly designed to keep unsuspecting visitors away, or perhaps a side effect of the jamming device."

"Mr. Marshall, we are talking about a device located several million kilometers away from the planets it is protecting. And, from the way you described it, this planetoid is automated?"

"Correct, Captain. At least, that is my assumption."

"Why wouldn't we see the planets with our planetary observation outposts? Or the old-style observation units? What were they called?"

"Telescopes, Captain," Robert Goldman supplied for Traynor.

"Thank you, Commander," Traynor acknowledged. He looked at Marshall questioningly.

"I can only assume that the device is somehow able to prevent it," Marshall answered.

"But that would mean . . . " Robert Goldman began.

"Correct, Commander," Marshall said. "The

enemy has had space flight for over a century longer than the Republic. And not just the experimental stage. Constructive space travel."

"Let me get this straight," Commander Dron Svenson said. "This thing is man-made?"

"Artificially created were my exact words," Marshall replied. "We don't know if the creatures that created this are, in fact, human."

"But if they can hide their home planets from our sensors," Robert Goldman asked, "why can't they hide their ships?"

"I can only guess," Marshall said, "that the equipment used must be immense, and they have not developed a way of miniaturizing it to a size useful on a starship."

"Captain," Kran interrupted. "Call from security."

Traynor nodded and thumbed the switch on his chair console.

"Yes, Commander?"

"Trouble in engineering, sir," Mark Carter's voice sounded worried. Instantly Traynor was alert.

"What is it?"

"Don't know, but I sent a squad to investigate. Something about an engineer going berserk."

Traynor slammed his palm against his thigh. "Dammit, what the hell is going on?!" The bridge crew was diplomatically quiet. "Get me that security squad!" Traynor commanded the communications officer. Major Kran's appendages fairly flew across the controls.

"Lieutenant Johnson here," was the Pronethan's reward.

"Johnson, this is the Captain," Traynor interrupted quickly. "Who's in charge?"

"Lieutenant Nater," the young man answered.

"Get him!" was the command. In the corridor, the

Mimnite jumped to carry out the captain's orders.

The six security men were split on either side of the open automatic doors to engineering. Johnson, Peter Trout, and Rene Millerand were against one, the corridor wall on one side of the door. Nater, Clancy O'Hanrahan, and Fred Peterson were in similar positions on the other side of the opening. Johnson waved to the Ganymedan, nearest the opening.

"Captain on the intercom." Nater nodded and, after careful maneuvering so as not to expose himself to possible fire from the man inside, moved the two meters to the nearby wall intercom.

"Nater."

"Situation, Hal." Traynor's voice, though as commanding as always, had a touch of anxiety in it.

"Colonel Corensky has a laser and has taken over the engineering section," Nater reported.

"Corensky? Why"

"Don't know, but he's blockaded himself on the upper deck with a clear view of the entrance. And he turned off the intercoms up there."

"No way up?"

"No."

"What about the others in there?"

"It seems everyone on the lower deck was let go. Only three officers were allowed on the upper deck. From what I can piece together, those on the lower level heard a loud crack, and a moment later O'Leery came flying over the railing from the upper deck."

"How is he?"

"Don't know. Corensky wouldn't let him be helped. We can see him lying there. Every once in a while he moves slightly.

"As for McKinley," Nater continued. "He knocked her out and propped her on the steps, blocking the only way up."

"What about cutting through?" Traynor asked.

"There's more, Alex," Nater said slowly. "He's got Erica as a hostage."

"What? I'm on my way." Traynor snapped. A second voice came over the intercom.

"No you aren't, Traynor."

"Nelson, what are you doing?" Traynor's voice sounded as though he had moved away from the speaker. Then the intercom went dead.

Immediately Nater tried to reach the chief of security. However, the intercom would not work.

"Johnson, try that intercom!" Nater called down the corridor. Johnson hit the switch, with no response. He shook his head at Nater, who immediately pulled O'Hanrahan aside.

"Get to Carter! Tell him something's up on the bridge. Colonel Nelson's involved. I'd assume there's at least one laser up there. Intercoms are out." The Ioan nodded and hurried to the nearest elevator. He punched the button, but nothing happened. He looked to Nater.

"Use the ladders!" Nater snapped. O'Hanrahan took off on the run. Nater turned back to the engineering section.

"What do we do not?" Trout asked.

"We wait," was Nater's response.

On the bridge, the reason for the abrupt end to the intercom connection to engineering was the service lasers being held by Nelson, N'goto, Spencer, and Peters.

Nelson ordered Kran to cut off all intercom communication. N'goto immediately neutralized the computerized controls of the elevators, which, unknown to the security detail, explained the lack of response when Clancy O'Hanrahan punched the elevator controls.

"What's the big idea, Nelson?" demanded the angry captain. Both Dron Svenson and David Lornton made moves toward *Polaris*'s executive officer, but N'goto's laser sufficiently quelled the idea.

"Plot us out of here, Victoria," Nelson ordered. He motioned Traynor away from the command chair, then seated himself there. "Implement, Ben."

"What's going on?" Traynor repeated. *Polaris* executed a smooth turn, and headed back the way it had come. Still, Nelson did not answer Traynor's questions. It was not until the ship had again passed through the radiation belt put out by the artificial asteroid that Nelson turned to Traynor.

"This, Captain, and I use the term loosely, is the forcible implementation of Space Service Regulation Book Four, Section Seven, Paragraph One." Nelson explained.

"The four-seven-one failed, Nelson, or are you too stupid to realize that?"

Nelson's face turned scarlet at Traynor's words.

"Don't cross me now, Traynor!" he yelled. "Or you won't make it to the review board!" He stopped and laughed, calming quickly. "Besides, it was all done according to regulations. Paragraph Two of that same section, and I quote . . . "

"I know the regs," Traynor informed the man. "Who were the substitutes, and what were the reasons?"

"Why, the chief pilot and navigator." Nelson smiled. "What other logical choices could be made? As for reasons for the substitution; obviously Majors Kran and De Gaulle are not emotionally capable of rendering an unbiased decision in this matter."

"I see," said Traynor. Standing between the pilot and navigation console, he cast a quick glance toward the two weapons officers standing behind and to

Nelson's right. As quick as the glance was, it did not go unnoticed.

"Don't try anything," warned Nelson. "I'd just as soon shoot you as take you back."

"Why, Nelson?" Traynor asked.

"Why? You're really asking why?" Nelson smiled again. "Because you've put this ship and its loyal crew in jeopardy ever since you took over. That thing at Station Fifteen. Now this little side trip while disobeying orders. You planned this from the moment you read the orders to head for Mimnon. It was your idea to search for the enemy fleet. And, jeopardizing this ship, you did."

"The ship wasn't in jeopardy," Traynor began.

"You don't call following a fleet of indeterminate size in one ship jeopardy?" Nelson said loudly.

"If they picked us up at all, which I'm sure they didn't, they probably thought we were a reflection of one of their ships on their sensors."

"What do you hope to gain, Colonel?" asked Maria McMasters from her position in front of the navigation console. Victoria Spencer's laser was trained on her.

"Gain? Why, this ship. I should have had it in the first place! I've put ten years on this ship! All the way from weapons officer to exec! An then they bring in some golden boy to take my job! One who coddles to the outworlders. And an Earther at that!"

"That's it, isn't it, Nelson!" Goldman exploded. "You've had it in for the Captain from the beginning because he wasn't a member of your precious Earth First party!"

"Easy, Goldman," warned Traynor.

"Yes, Commander, tread softly," said Nelson. "But, you have judged the point correctly. Traynor became a problem when we learned he was not a member of the Loyal Earth party."

The four stopped in front of the elevator doors. The three Vendrans looked questioningly at the fourth man, Commander Mark Carter.

"What now?" Travis Dralen questioned. "The elevators aren't working."

"This is the only way to the bridge," Carter answered. "Take too long to cut through from any other point. This entrance is directly under the bridge elevator doors. Because there is only one entrance to the bridge, the ship's designers put a ladder in the elevator tube from this point up."

"How do we get the door open?" Branor Colare asked. "We didn't bring any heavy cutters along, and those small cutters you have won't make a dent in the doors."

"Oh come now, Branor," Carter laughed, even in the seriousness of the situation. Fedar Mohand, the third Vendran, joined in the laughter.

As the others watched, Mohand carefully gripped one side of the two-piece sliding door, at the joint in the middle. Straining against the lock mechanism, Mohand slowly produced a gap in the door. Even the two Vendrans standing with Carter were amazed at the incredible show of strength by their companion. Carter, though in awe of the raw power exhibited by Mohand, was not surprised. He had come to expect this kind of demonstration from Mohand.

Standing one hundred seventy-nine centimeters, and weighing one hundred fifteen kilos, Mohand was the largest Vendran Carter had ever met. Legs the size of tree trunks, arms thicker than Carter's legs, Mohand was by far the strongest member of the *Polaris* crew. If there was a job requiring brute strength, Mohand was the man. Not to take away from his intelligence. The

Vendran was studying for a psychology security rating, which would qualify Mohand as a potential squad leader.

And Carter needed more qualified squad leaders. Out of eighty-five security men, only six had passed the psychology test, and Nater wasn't much use anymore, what with his new duties as captain's aide.

But it was Mohand's brawn that Carter needed now. And the Vendran succeeded in the task. Taxing his powerful muscles to the limit, the brawny security man was able to pull the doors apart. When he finally stepped away, the doors looked as if hydraulic grippers had done the job.

"Excellent, Fedar," Carter said.

"Shucks, chief," Mohand grinned in mock humility. " 'Twas nothing." The others laughed, though whether it was from the joking interplay, or to mask the anxious feelings they were having, even they didn't know.

"OK, we go up the ladder," Carter said, bringing them back to reality. "Find a handhold and wait until everyone's up. I know it'll crowded, but that's life.

"Shouldn't have any problem with the doors from the inside. Just use the electro-cutters on the locking mechanisms, and they'll spring open.

"We don't know how many lasers, or who's involved, so if in doubt, stun. Not the Captain, though. And remember," Carter stressed. "We go together."

They nodded. Branor Colare was the first to reach for the ladder.

As Fedar Mohand was demonstrating his herculean strength to his security compatriots on "A" deck, another security detail was dealing with their problem in engineering.

Nater's crew had felt the course change and

wondered about it. O'Hanrahan had returned, informing them that Carter was seeing to the bridge problem personally. Corensky fired an occasional laser blast when one of the security men slipped up and showed himself at the door.

It was a stalemate. Corensky could not leave or move around, but the security detail could not enter or get a clear shot at him.

And then there were the hostages. One with a possible broken back, one with unknown injuries, and Major Erica LeMay, who, at any moment, the crazed Corensky could burn. A girl who, two months earlier, would have been a petrified mass of hysteria.

"I've got it!" Trout exclaimed. The others were surprised to see the wide smile on his face.

"Spill it, man!" Johnson demanded. Nater looked at him hard, and the cold eyes of the big man were demanding.

"OK," Trout began quickly. "If I could, I'd dash across and get against the wall between the lower and upper decks. We Vendrans move fast, you know." His little joke was not well received. "But I can't," he continued at an even quicker pace. "Because the Colonel has my start, namely the entrance, well covered. But what if . . . " And the Vendran outlined his plan to the listens. As he finished, Nater nodded slowly.

"It's a long shot," the Ganymedan said. "And dangerous. But it just might work. Sure you want to do this, Peter?" The Vendran nodded, strapping his laser to his belt. He tucked the stunner inside his shirt.

"It's your play," Nater said. "Whenever you're ready?"

Trout took a deep breath and trotted down the corridor some twenty meters. He stretched his legs, took a second deep breath, and relaxed a bit. He checked both legs carefully, then waved to the others that he was ready.

"Now!" he yelled, and exploded into motion, sprinting toward the others at full speed.

On Trout's call to action, Nater and Millerand, on either side of the entrance to engineering, began firing continuous stunner blasts in the direction of the barricaded Chief engineer. Corensky ducked at their first blast.

Trout veered into the room, and the moment he flashed through the doors, he knew he'd never run faster in his life. He also knew it hadn't been fast enough. He felt the laser burn across his legs as he shot into a dive toward the far wall. At the speed he was moving, it was impossible to stop quickly. Consequently, the little Vendran slammed heavily into the wall, knocking his breath out for a second. His highly conditioned body recovered quickly, and he began a quick check of his body to see that everything was still functioning correctly. The laser burns were minor, but hurt like the devil.

The stunner fire was keeping Corensky under cover, and he knew that at least one man was on the lower level. It was only a matter of time before they got him. But, Corensky smiled to himself, not before I get rid of the LeMay woman.

As if she read his mind, Erica realized that if she was to live much longer, she'd have to make her move now. She grabbed for his wrist with both hands, striving to push the laser away. Corensky laughed and slapped her with his free hand. The Europan tumbled backwards. She closed her eyes tightly as Corensky took careful aim. When she didn't feel the laser slice through her, she peeked through one eye. Standing before her was Peter Trout, a laser in his hand. Vladimir Corensky lay on the floor between herself and Trout, a fist-sized hole in his head. Hal Nater was climbing the stairway.

"You OK, Erica?" Nater asked concernedly.

"Yeah, I think so," she answered. "Don't worry about me. See to Shawn and Charlene."

"Fred, get some sickbay people down here!" Nater called.

"Why don't you use the intercom?" Erica asked.

"It's been shut off," explained Nater. "Something's happening on the bridge."

Alexander Traynor shook his head at Lieutenant David Lornton, who had risen from his seat and was slowly inching toward the command chair. Traynor shrugged toward Victoria Spencer, who, while performing her duties as navigator, was also covering Maria McMasters with a service laser. Lornton nodded, understanding. He returned to his seat.

"You know, Traynor," Nelson smiled, baiting the captain. "It won't be so bad. Of course you'll probably lose a couple of ranks, but I don't think they'll dump you completely. Probably give you a desk job on some planetary outpost." Nelson laughed, though never taking his eyes off Traynor. "You'll never command a ship again.

"And, while you're at your little desk, be thinking of how I'm running this ship. Like it should be run."

"So you'll run this ship the way it should be run," Traynor said, sarcastically.

"That's right!" Nelson roared, coming to his feet. "I'll put these outworlders in their place. Show them who's boss."

"Sounds as if you consider yourself better than we outworlders," Robert Goldman commented. "I suppose you consider Earthers the master race, from which all others came?"

"That's right, outworlder. Earthers are the masters, and should be treated as such!"

"Historically speaking, advocates of the master-race syndrome tend to live short lives," Marshall said quietly. "And die violently. A prime example would be Adolf Hitler of twentieth-century Germany, on Earth."

Carl Nelson swung on the Triton, and was preparing an appropriate answer when Danart N'goto interrupted.

"Something coming up behind us. Fast."

"What is it?" Nelson demanded.

"Two ships, destroyers. They're firing on us."

Polaris was rocked by disruptor blasts. Carl Nelson, off balance where he was standing, was thrown into the captain. Knowing this was his only chance, Traynor took it, smashing a forearm into his exec's chest while gripping Nelson's wrist with his other hand.

David Lornton launched himself in a dive only a Vendran could complete, flashing the three meters between himself and Victoria Spencer in the blink of an eye, and smashing the hand with the laser into the console.

As if on cue, the doors to the elevator sprung open and the four security men, led by Mark Carter, exploded onto the bridge to add to the confusion. N'goto and Peters tried to bring their lasers to bear, but they were immediately cut down by the newcomers' stunners.

Traynor and Nelson rolled on the deck between the tank and the pilot/navigation consoles. Neither could gain an advantage. The laser hummed once.

"Arrrrr!" Traynor cried.

Maria McMasters screamed, horrified. A huge hole had appeared in Traynor's left arm. The others moved to aid the captain, but before they could help, it was all over.

As if the pain of the laser blast spurred him on, Traynor fought like a caged animal. He smashed a hard blow to Nelson's midsection, causing the older man to gasp for breath. As Nelson rolled off, the captain quickly followed up his brief advantage with two hard rights to the jaw. Nelson collapsed to the floor.

"Captain, you're hurt!" McMasters cried as Traynor stood up.

"Station, Commander." Traynor ordered weakly. She sat back down. Goldman was at his controls. Traynor staggered to the command console and sat down, grimacing in pain.

"Kran, Marshall, get everything working. I want section reports. Call battle stations. Situation?"

"Two destroyers on us, sir," reported the Triton. A laser blast, though dissipated on the shields of the *Polaris*, still rocked the ship. "Sensor reading an indeterminable number of others at extreme range, following the destroyers. Estimated time until they catch us: three point six-five minutes."

"Weapons?"

"Everything at peak operation, Captain," Dron Svenson answered quickly. Traynor nodded weakly and spun his chair to address the two in front. He was in time to see Fedar Mohand lift the still limp body of Carl Nelson and sling it easily across his broad shoulders. The others had already been escorted off the bridge by the security men.

"Captain, engineering and sickbay on the lines." Kran reported.

"Engineering first."

"This is Hal, Captain. Everything secure. A lady told me to tell you to prepare for a surprise."

Traynor smiled in spite of the pain. "Now or later?"

"The lady says both," Nater laughed.

"Thanks, Hal," Traynor said softly. He cut the Ganymedan off before Nater could become modest about the accomplishment. The bridge crew could feel the tenseness leave the captain.

"Mr. Goldman, accelerate to full emergency speed, then prepare to accelerate again, on my command."

"Aye, sir!" Goldman answered quickly, though not understanding the order completely.

"Alex," came from the intercom. "De Gaulle here."

"How are my people, Marc?"

"O'Leery's got a broken hip. Two places. Be a while before he's dancing a jig." The ship rocked as a disruptor blast was dissipated on the shields. "McKinley has a shattered jaw, plus a concussion."

"One minute, forty-five seconds until enemy fleet within effective firing range of their guns," Marshall interrupted.

"Take care of them," Traynor told the doctor. He was about to sign off, but De Gaulle got in his last piece of information.

"Corensky was burned. Trout had to."

"I'll take your word for now, and review it later. Traynor out." He thumbed the intercom again.

"Engineering, Nater."

"Hal, what's Erica say?"

"I'll put her on broadcast, Captain."

A moment later Erica LeMay's voice sounded on the intercom.

"What is it, Alex? I'm busy."

"What about the engines?"

"Be ready in a moment."

"One minute, five seconds," Marshall sang out.

"You've got less than a minute."

"No problem."

"Fifty-five seconds."

"Would you please hurry?"

"I'm only one woman, Alex!"

"Forty-five seconds."

"Listen, snap it up!"

"I can only do so much at once. This walking high rise and his pals are useless to me down here."

"Twenty-five seconds."

"Miss LeMay, anything you ever wanted is yours!"

"Fifteen seconds."

"Finished. Go!"

"Accelerate, Goldman!" Traynor fairly screamed.

Polaris jumped as Goldman poured the new-found power into the engines. The pilot stared at his controls in disbelief.

"Sir, something's wrong with my controls. They read us moving at over two hundred fifty BK's." Goldman used the standard abbreviation for billions of kilometers per hour as he spoke to the captain. "Now two-sixty, two-seventy, two-eighty. It's impossible! We're over three hundred Bk's!"

Traynor grinned at him. "How's our pursuit?" he asked Marshall, who stood bent over the science station.

"Falling behind, sir," the Triton grinned. "Very quickly." His grin faded as fast as it had appeared. "Picking up a large group of ships. Ahead of us."

"How large?" Traynor demanded instantly.

"Very large!" came the emphatic reply.

"Looks like we'll have to fight after all," Traynor said, resignedly. "Battle stations. Prepare evasive maneuvers. Get your section primed, Svenson."

"Sir," Major Kran interrupted. "Message from the new fleet. Admiral Antonozzi in *Agincourt*. They're ours, sir."

Traynor smiled, breathing a huge sigh of relief. The bridge crew let out a cheer as the ships of the Republic came into view on the large visiscreen.

"Identify us and tell them we're going home. Marshall, feed 'em what we've got on the enemy."

"Aye, sir," Kran and Marshall called out together.

The main visiscreen became filled with the images of the ships of the Republic's fleet.

"Look at 'em!" an excited Goldman exclaimed. "There's *Agincourt, Jutland, Buenos Aires, New Troy, Okinawa.* Must be thirty or forty battleships out there."

"Fifty-two." Marshall corrected. "Twenty nine heavy cruisers, forty-five cruisers, and a large number of the smaller classes."

"That many?" Traynor asked.

"I'd estimate at least eighty-five percent of the Barnard fleet."

"Really?" Traynor said. As the bridge crew watched, he slowly collapsed. The last thing he remembered was Kran calling De Gaulle to the bridge.

VII

"I never have liked review boards," Shawn O'Leery grumbled. "They take forever making decisions. And then you find out they've been deciding whether to go out to eat, or have it sent in."

" 'Tis the truth, Shawn, me lad," Peter Trout mimicked the Ioan's accent.

"Knock it off, you guys," Hal Nater commanded. He flipped his head toward a figure seated in a corner of the large conference room. Erica LeMay's face betrayed no emotion. "Some of us are worried."

The four, along with eight of their *Polaris* companions, were waiting in the conference room, aboard Orbital Station Fifteen. They had been delivered to Station Fifteen over six hours earlier by special station transport. It was the second day the review board had listened to testimony on the incidents aboard the USR *Polaris*.

Nine days had passed since the battle of Alpha Centauri. In a massive display of force, the USR Fleet had totally annihilated the defensive capabilities of the enemy fleet, while suffering reasonable, even considered small, losses in comparison. The two planets of the system were surrounded and forced to surrender.

When the first ground forces of the USR landed on the planets, it was discovered that two different races of creatures lived on the planets. The outer planet, approximately the size of Mars of the Sol system, was inhabited by creatures similar to, in appearance, though internally somewhat different from, troopers of the USR. These people welcomed the coming of the USR with open arms, for it was discovered these humanoid creatures had been the slaves of the creatures from the other planet for over ten centuries. Their planet, Darsinia, was eager to throw off the oppressive rule of the Ralupdrans, as the creatures of the other planet were known.

The second planet, the interior of the two, measured a near-equal to Jupiter. Its atmosphere was composed largely of chlorine gas, as the Republic's scientists had predicted after examining the remains of the starship *Polaris* had brought in. The planet's gravity was equal to twice the gravity of Earth. Therefore, the first troops to be sent to the planet's surface were Vendrans. The Vendrans were able to move with no difficulty in the high gravity. Though the atmosphere was both poisonous and impossible to see in, the protective suits the USR troopers wore, with their sophisticated electronic equipment, made the mens' job relatively simple. Two battalions of troops landed and took control of the Ralupdran government.

The creatures of Ralupdra were large reptilian creatures, fearsome creatures that reminded the Republic soldiers of their history lessons on the prehistoric dinosaurs of ancient Earth.

The higher-echelon officials of the Republic landed next, to discuss terms of surrender with the officials of the Ralupdrans. During the discussions, it was learned that many of the Ralupdrans had been actively opposing continuation of the war. The people were against it, and had been for more than a century. The military and the hereditary leaders of Ralupdra continued the interstellar conflict over the objections of the people.

The victorious fleet, leaving a sizable sub-fleet as the representative of the Republic and a deterrent to any further action by the Ralupdrans, made its way home to the Barnard system. High-ranking officials of Fleet Command remained on the two planets of the Alpha

Centauri system to work with the friendly officials there. One admiral, seeing a long-range goal in the talks beginning on Ralupdra, voiced the opinion that, if the Ralupdrans became a part of the Republic, transplanted Ralupdrans would be an immense breakthrough for the Republic in the mining colonies on Kappa Barnard.

There was rejoicing throughout the member worlds of the Republic, the likes of which had never been seen before, when news of the end of the space war was transmitted. Businesses, governments, whole planets, came to a standstill for the celebration. The Interplanetary Council, in a landmark unanimous decision, proclaimed the day a holiday throughout the Republic.

There remained the matter of *Polaris.* Immediately upon the return of the fleet, a review board was called. Staff General Adamson, wearing the four stars of his rank, sat as chief administrator of the board. Adamson, the supreme commander of the Service forces in the Barnard system, assembled six officers to serve with him; all of the rank of admiral or higher. Rear Admiral Antonozzi, because of the one star he wore, was not asked to sit on the board.

Computer tapes of much of the incident aboard *Polaris* were presented to the board. Each of the surviving senior officers of the *Polaris* was interviewed, and their testimony recorded. Junior members of the crew, selected because of their intimacy with the incident, were interviewed by the board. It had taken the better part of the six hours the group now gathered had spent on Station Fifteen for the interviews. Mark Carter had been the last, dismissed from the board room fifteen minutes earlier.

A sideline to the review board was the ruling by Staff General Adamson that Peter Trout's shooting of Corensky was justifiable. It was a ruling all viewed as favorable to the overall case before the board.

Shawn O'Leery lifted himself to his one good leg and reached for his crutches. His left leg, the one with the broken hip, was in a cast from ankle to well above his waist. He had hobbled to the hangar deck immediately upon being released from sick bay. As the maintenance crews gathered around to listen to his story, Myra Shanesey, who had been with him a great deal of her off-duty time, jokingly mentioned that they were planning on erecting a statue on the nose of one of the LC's, and he was the first applicant for the job. Even O'Leery had to laugh with the others.

Now the Ioan turned to the other member of the walking wounded.

"Can I get ye somethin'?" O'Leery asked Charlene McKinley. The girl shook her head.

The only response she could make was by shaking or nodding her head. Her jaw, fractured in several places and broken cleanly in two, had been wired shut by the doctors. That part of the operation, though they were dealing with a number of fractures, was relatively simple. The concussion she suffered was more serious than they had originally thought. McKinley had remained unconscious for two days before she woke up. Her first words to Marc De Gaulle, written on a note pad he provided, were to complain of the worst hangover in her life.

O'Leery was halfway across the conference room when the door of the adjacent room, where the review board was in session, opened.

Alexander Traynor, his injured arm in a sling, exited from the board room. His face was a mask, with no emotion readable. Erica LeMay was the first to rush to him.

"What's the verdict, Alex?" she asked, gripping his good arm tightly.

"How'd it go, Captain?" Shawn O'Leery hobbled up.

"Yeah." "What'd they say?" "Did we win?"

"Let's go back to *Polaris*," was all Traynor said. He refused to answer any questions they put to him. He sat silently during the shuttle ride to the *Polaris*. Traynor quickly passed waiting crewmen, eager for news about the review board's decision. The captain's companions merely shrugged their collective shoulders, telling the others they were equally mystified.

Traynor hurried to an intercom on the hanger deck. He contacted the bridge.

"Commander Vlres, put me on shipwide," Traynor ordered. A moment passed, then Vlres informed the captain he was patched shipwide.

"This is Captain Traynor speaking. The following people are to be in conference room 'A' in five minutes." He began rattling off names. "Majors Francis Jenkins, Kran, Erica LeMay, and Theodore Marshall. Commanders Mark Carter, Reg Dickson, Robert Goldman, Charlene McKinley, Maria McMasters, Mildred Makem, Todd Michaels, Shawn O'Leery, Dron Svenson, and Vlres. Lieutenants David Lornton, Harold Nater, and Peter Trout. Traynor out."

The gathered throng waited patiently as the five-minute mark came and passed. Among themselves they discussed what reasons Traynor could possibly have to call the meeting.

Silence was immediate when Alexander Traynor entered the room. Each member of the crew came to attention as the captain went directly to the head of the conference table. He set the large satchel, that had travelled from Station Fifteen to *Polaris* under his arm, on the table.

Traynor began. "Commanders Dickson, Makem, and Michaels." He reached into the satchel and removed three envelopes. Everyone in the room recognized what they were immediately. "Your new orders. The shuttle to Station Fifteen leaves in one hour. Dismissed." Stunned, the four officers picked up their packets and left quickly.

"At ease, everyone," Traynor smiled. "Have a seat." He punched the intercom at the head of the table. "Stuart, is that you?" He received an affirmative answer. "Put this on shipwide. All activity, except absolutely necessary, suspended."

"Aye, sir," came the Lunarite's voice. "Shipwide, sir."

"Ladies and gentlemen, this is Captain Traynor. This is a special occasion for *Polaris* and its crew. For the special role *Polaris* played in the recent action of the fleet, a special commendation is being prepared for each member of the crew. I wanted to let you know of this important occurence. That is why I suspended all activity.

"On to the next item of business. Because of incidents aboard *Polaris* recently, a review board was commissioned, presided over by Staff General Adamson. I'm sure everyone is familiar with the incidents. Therefore, I see no need to rehash old news.

"The findings of the board have caused a number of vacancies aboard *Polaris*. Officers that you knew and-well, they won't be back.

"Before I tell you of their replacements, I'm reminded that I have a number of special commendations, which I will present personally at a later time. These commendations, for bravery, will be presented to Lieutenants Colare, Dralen, Johnson, Millerand, Mohand, O'Hanrahan, and Peterson, for their actions in the recent internal problems aboard *Polaris*. Congratulations, gentlemen." He paused for a moment, then continued.

"Commander Mark Carter, for your actions in the recent incidents, and your complete control of the situation, the board accepted the recommendation for your promotion to the rank of Major, and your continuance as chief security officer. Will you accept?"

"Aye, sir!" The Oberonite's face, normally emotionless, was all smiles. Traynor tossed him an envelope the captain had removed from the satchel. It contained Major's stripes and insignia.

"Congratulations." Traynor paused, then began again. "Lieutenant Peter Trout, in recognition of your conspicuous heroism, the board accepted the recommendation for your promotion to commander, and your appointment to the newly created position of assistant security officer. Do you accept?"

"Aye, sir!" Trout exclaimed. A packet was produced for him.

"Congratulations. Commander Dron Svenson, the board also accepted the recommendation for your promotion to major, and your continuance as weapons officer. Do you accept?" Svenson, speechless, nodded. His packet appeared.

"Congratulations. Lieutenant David Lornton, the board accepted the recommendation for your promotion to commander, and your appointment to the newly created position of assistant weapons officer. Do you accept?" Lornton answered affirmatively and received his packet.

Traynor continued with his impromptu ceremony. McKinley became a major and the assistant chief engineer. O'Leery, also a new major, became the new chief engineer. Vlres, McMasters, and Goldman were promoted to major, and were made the heads of communications, navigation, and pilots respectively. Then came Marshall.

"Major Theodore Marshall, for your major role in the ending of the interstellar war the Republic has been waging for the past centuries, the board accepted the recommendation for your promotion to the rank of colonel, and your appointment to the position of science officer of *Polaris*. Do you accept?"

"Yes, sir, I do," the lean Triton replied. His packet appeared as quickly as had the others.

"Congratulations. Also, commendations from the independent governments of the Republic, the Interplanetary Council, and the General of the Service himself, will be arriving for you soon. Again congratulations."

"Thank you, sir," the man answered happily.

"Major Kran, the board accepted the recommendation for your promotion to colonel, and your appointment to the position of executive officer of *Polaris*. Do you accept?"

"Yes, Captain, I do," Kran answered. As with the others, the Pronethan's packet was tossed before her.

"Congratulations," Traynor said. Slowly he turned to Erica LeMay, seated to his immediate right. The Europan girl was sitting stiffly in her chair, not knowing what to expect. Already she had been relieved of her post. Perhaps she would receive her travelling orders. She didn't believe Traynor would do that, but there was no position left for her.

"Major Erica LeMay, in recognition of your recent achievements, and your actions during the recent incidents aboard *Polaris*, and after some deliberation, the board accepted the recommendation for your promotion to the rank of captain, and your appointment as commander of the USR *Polaris*. Do you accept?" He grinned at her, caught totally surprised by his announcement. The others in the room were equally as surprised.

"Do you accept?" Traynor asked again.

"I s-s-suppose so," she stuttered.

"You suppose?" he raised a questioning eyebrow, his eyes underneath twinkling.

More confidently, she answered his question. "Yes, I accept."

"Good," Traynor said. He tossed a packet to her.

"Congratulations, Captain."

In amazement, Erica poured the contents onto the table. It was captain's braids and bars. She looked from one surprised face at the table to another. Then she turned to Traynor.

"What about you?" she asked. "What happens to . . . " Traynor cut her off with a wave of his hand. He began fishing into the satchel again. Out came two more packets. He tossed one to Nater, seated immediately to his left.

"This one's yours, Hal."

Nater poured the contents onto the table. Major's stripes and insignia. The huge Ganymedan was surprised, but pleasantly so. He turned to thank Traynor and ask what his new job was, but fell silent as he watched Traynor slowly open the last packet and pour the contents onto the table.

Four objects slid from the packet. Two were five centimeter stripes, to be worn on the sleeve. The other objects were collar pins. Each pin had two stars set on it.

"These," Traynor grinned, speaking loudly. "Are mine!"

Erica laughed with joy. An admiral. And not just a rear admiral. A full fledged admiral. She was even happier for Alex than she had been for herself. Then a sobering thought hit her.

"This means you'll be leaving *Polaris*," she said, struggling to hold back the tears. Traynor stepped to her. Slowly she stood, looking into her eyes.

"Now, now, *ma cherie*, why are you so quick to be rid of me?" he asked, putting his arms around her.

"I don't understand," she said.

"Obviously," he answered, laughing.

"Explain yourself now!" she ordered. "You're speaking to the captain of this ship now."

"Well, well. Feisty, aren't we?" he said. She gave

him a look that he knew meant business. He continued quickly to soothe her ruffled feathers. "My assistant," he nodded towards Nater, "and I will be aboard *Polaris* for quite a while. You see, you might call it my flagship."

"Flagship?"

"Of my fleet. Of one!" he laughed. The rest of the assembled group, having been diplomatically quiet, began talking at once.

"Doing what?" LeMay made herself heard over the noise.

"You might call it public relations," Traynor answered in the same tone. "The fleet brass thinks people will want to meet me, along with the members of the crew that brought about the end of the space war. My opinion is that they won't, but my opinion is worth nothing against the opinions of the brass."

The gathered members of the crew began crowding around, congratulating the new captain and admiral, and themselves.

It was a party to end all parties; a celebration to beat all celebrations. It began in the crew lounge, but quickly spilled out into the corridors. The central distribution unit was hard pressed to keep food and drinks in abundant numbers. Private stocks were broken out, and the finest of the fine liquors in the Republic were passed around for the enjoyment of the partygoers. Every member of the crew made an appearance at the party at one time or another.

A great deal of backslapping and hearty congratulations were passed among the members of the crew. Everybody had something complementary or jokingly sarcastic to say about the new promotions, but each crew member made a point of congratulating the new captain of *Polaris* on her promotion. She thanked each member individually, and under Traynor's approving eyes, tried to address each crewman by his or her name. She made mistakes, but they were few in relation to the number of crewmen aboard *Polaris.*

And when it was over, four weary officers were all who remained in the previously crowded room.

"What's going to happen to the fearsome foursome?" Marc De Gaulle asked.

"N'goto and Peters are headed for the Ariel penal colony. Too bad, too. N'goto could have been a good officer. He was a fine scientist. Did a good job when he was away from Nelson."

"Thank you, but no thank you. I'll take Marshall as my science officer any day," the new captain of the *Polaris*, Erica LeMay, exclaimed.

"Absolutely. No comparison." agreed Traynor. "Still, if he hadn't gotten involved with Nelson . . . " His sentence trailed off.

"Speaking of Nelson," newly promoted Major Hal Nater asked quietly. "What of him? What'd the board decide?" The huge Ganymedan shifted his massive frame, searching for a comfortable position. In frustration, he finally rose to his full two-plus meters. "Think now that I'm a major I can have a chair built to fit me?" The others laughed at his discomfort, a legend aboard *Polaris.*

"We'll see what we can do," laughed Erica.

The light laughter passed as they returned to more serious thoughts.

"Nelson cracked," Traynor informed them. "Totally and completely. Such a sad sight."

"Sad?!" exclaimed De Gaulle loudly. "Man, the fool shot you. A few centimeters to the right and you wouldn't be here!"

"I know, Marc," nodded Traynor. "Still, it's sad to see a man lose himself right in front of you." De Gaulle thought about it for a moment, then nodded agreeably.

"Anyway, he's headed for the mental rehabilitation center on Ceres. Spencer too." he added. "She's OK, just wants to be with him. Help him. In her own way, I think she loved him."

Erica LeMay nodded. She was a woman. She understood Spencer's feelings.

They sat, or stood, quietly, each with his or her own thoughts. It was Marc De Gaulle who broke the silence.

"Must you be so tall?" he cried loudly. "I get such a feeling of inadequacy!"

"That reminds me," Nater grinned good naturedly. "I must get around to having that talk with Major Upshaw soon."

"Oh Geez!" A look of alarm crossed De Gaulle's face.

"What is it, doctor?" Erica asked, her face lit with concern.

"Marge! I told her I'd meet her fifteen minutes ago!" He jumped up. "We're, uh, doing some research on cellular structure," he threw back at them as he made his way quickly to the exit.

Nater turned to the seated couple.

"If you will excuse me, I too have an engagement." Elaborating no further, he headed for the door.

Traynor turned to look at LeMay.

"Well, Captain?"

"Well, Admiral?"

"Conversationalists you're not!" came from the door. They both turned to see Nater's huge form slowly disappear as the automatic doors closed. Erica blushed a deep red. Traynor turned back to her, chuckling softly.

"He's right, you know."

"True," she answered. "I never was much of a conversationalist." Then she smiled.